The Shooter

By

Vincent A. Simonelli

ISBN: 1-4107-0950-7 (e-book)
ISBN: 1-4107-0951-5 (Paperback)

This book is printed on acid free paper.

1stBooks - rev. 02/11/03

Chapter One

Hoffman Muir

April 3, 1997 - New Orleans

A cool, driving rain blew in from across the bayou, blinding drivers and soaking streets. Along the river, rows of metal-sided warehouses being pelted by sheets of water were shaking under the pressure of the ferocious winds.

Inside one of the buildings two men sat alone among the open crates and smashed cardboard boxes of some long abandoned enterprise. The sound of the rain was nearly deafening. Fernando Cabrerra twitched nervously in his seat as he eyed the man who sat across from him.

Cabrerra was a Cuban exile who came to the United States when Castro closed the casinos, throwing hundreds of low level bagmen, pimps, callgirls and hoods out of work. Cabrerra had been an enforcer for organized crime interests operating out of the Copa.

Once in the States he had become involved with efforts to free his homeland. He helped organize former Cubans for a paramilitary group that evolved into Brigade 2506, the group that had "invaded" Cuba at the Bay of Pigs. Later, still stinging from the defeat, he continued to train exiles with the help of CIA officials in the bayous outside New Orleans. When the FBI moved in to close down the training sites he was detained by authorities. By the spring of 1963 he was well known for his anti-Castro activities in New Orleans, including a noisy confrontation with Lee Harvey Oswald on a busy street corner that led to his second arrest.

Now in his late sixties, his strength sapped by an aggressive lifestyle, he was a small, tired man with striking silver hair and a dark wrinkled complexion.

"Senior, Muir, why have you brought me here? It has been a very long time."

Hoffman Muir was a tall hard man also in his late sixties, but trim and surprisingly fit. His salt and pepper hair was cut short and as he stood, you could see his six foot chiseled frame had hardly diminished with the years. Slowly, silently, he moved to a rust stained window and watched the rain pound the Mississippi beyond the pier.

He puffed on a short cigar, easing the smoke from his lungs, then turned towards Cabrerra.

"It has been too long. I'm afraid you're out of touch, Fernando. I haven't been Hoffman Muir for over thirty years."

"I did not know. But that doesn't change anything…why am I here." He rose from his seat in a defiant manner.

"I would appreciate it if you would sit down. I don't want to insist."

Cabrerra sat.

Muir walked back to the table and leaned over the shaken man.

"I need to know what you have been saying to Arliss. I know you've been seeing him."

"Nothing, my old friend." He was perspiring freely, tapping a finger on the table. "I saw him just once…last year. I told him nothing."

"What did he want to know, then?"

"He asked me only one question." A long pause as Cabrerra swallowed hard. "He asked me if I knew whether or not you were still alive."

Hoffman smiled and leaned back in his chair, his eyes fixed on the nervous collapsing man before him. "Go on."

"I did not know what to say. I had heard about Hayes death in Florida, but I knew nothing about you. Arliss…he was certain you would come after him if you knew he was writing that book...he was right, wasn't he?"

"A foolish question compadre."

The rain had begun to let up, but not enough to hear the gunshot as Cabrerra tried to make a run for the door. The second shot, as Hoffman stood over his already dead prey was meant to deliver a message.

Billy Petro

April 16, 1997 - Boston

The Kennedy library stands on the shores of Boston harbor, a glistening edifice of tinted glass and white concrete. It was almost nightfall and the museum was bustling. Limos, cars and taxis pulled up to the front of the building dropping off the well-dressed dignitaries of the city.

Tonight the library was hosting a reception commemorating the retirement of Warren Church, the long-time editor of the Boston Post. Tonight the city's elite would honor the man who hounded their every misstep for the last forty years, ending one of the longest reigns in American Journalistic history.

The crowd gathered inside the main foyer, a large open area bordered by tinted glass on three sides with a ceiling that rises four stories above their heads. Most attendees were in formal attire, passing amongst one another making small talk and pressing flesh.

Laying low, staring out at the harbor, a group of people ignored the buzz of activity around them. Only one wore a tux. Charlie "Silver" Fox had the pleasure of delivering the keynote speech tonight. For many years the Silver Fox and Warren Church were two of the most respected men in America; Church at the Post and Fox, as editor, at the Washington Sun.

Widely regarded as men of high integrity and honor they were ruthless in their pursuit of the truth bowing to no institution of government or no man of great wealth and power. Tonight, Church was stepping down just as his friend, Fox, had done seven months earlier in a similar fete in Washington.

For his part, Fox had gone into semi-retirement, having returned to the city where he grew up, purchasing the daily paper there. With no more windmills to conquer, no more dragons to slay, he had taken over the Everett Post-Dispatch in a small blue-collar city on the northern outskirts of Boston.

Tonight he would honor his friend and their profession with one last salute to his old colleague. As he went over his speech for the fiftieth time, in his mind, the gentle woman by his side, looked into his eyes, smiling. Claire Alere was his companion for these last thirty years. It was at her gentle insistence that he stepped down following a triple bypass operation and changes in the ownership that had left him tired and unsure of his future in the fourth estate.

She was happy to see him in the limelight, once again, and had insisted that his only reporter attend the ceremony, just to see him in action. The reporter, Billy "Petro" Petraconti, had followed Fox throughout his illustrious career, long ago having given up his dreams of emulating him. Now as a forty-five year old staff reporter for a daily paper that records the births and deaths in a small city, he found himself unenthused and empty.

He too, returned home after a time with a big city paper, only he came home scared, unsure and beaten. Twenty-two years ago, Billy's career was on the verge of taking off. He was a hot shot graduate from Syracuse working his way along the fast track at the Buffalo Chronicle when he stumbled upon a trail of corruption and power gone unchecked.

With the support of his Editor and the confidence of his youth, he relentlessly tracked down one city employee on the take after another. His stories appeared daily and he got his own column; The Billy Petro Report. Then after four months of solid investigative reporting it all came crashing down.

On a rainy night in July he received a call from one of the informants he had carefully culled from the city's payroll. The man had indicated an unusually high degree of urgency in meeting him at a distant locale, immediately. It was two in the morning and he thought he could feel a genuine crack in the final barriers placed between him and City Hall, itself. He decided to meet the man.

Despite the protests of his fiancé, he left. He was barely to his car when the entire front portion of his apartment building was blown away by a fiery explosion, knocking Billy unconscious and sending him half way across the street with cuts from the flying glass. His fiancée, Terry, never had a chance.

When he came to, he was in an emergency room. It was morning and his editor gave him the devastating news. Later that morning, he learned that his informant was found dead from a single gunshot to the head, an assumed suicide. Billy knew different. He was alive because he had been warned. He never found out if the informant had actually killed himself or not, but he assumed otherwise.

After Terry's death, he was unable to pick up the story. In fact, he was unable to write a word. A former classmate of his finished the stories, concluding that the informant was the highest level of corruption and responsible for Terry's murder. He and Billy had argued the point, but Billy lacked the inner strength to prevail.

A short time later, Billy moved back to Everett, taking the position of a one man news staff at the Post Dispatch, burying the memories and, for all intent and purpose, his hopes of a career in Journalism.

As he looked about the foyer, he saw all these men and women who were doing the things he longed to do. As it had so many times over these past twenty-two years, the aching returned. Billy stared silently into the harbor as darkness began to fall. He barely felt the light touch of the hand on his shoulder.

Alexandria Cortina, was an old friend of Billy's. She was a high school classmate of Billy and his best friend Pete Webster. The three had been together for as long as anyone in town could remember. It was Alex that had nursed Billy out of his abject depression and, eventually, got him the job at the Post Dispatch.

She taught at the local high school; English and Computer Sciences, having always been fascinated by the electronics boom and the information explosion that was escalating all around them. Alex was alone, but not lonely. She was too busy. Billy always told her she was too much of a "Renaissance Man" to be stuck in Everett, a place where change was never embraced, but took place only when the population was either cajoled, forced or hoodwinked.

For all her worldly interests, she loved Everett, it's people were warm and familiar; their lives uncomplicated and passionate. What it all boiled down to was that it was where her heart was. And that, for some inexplicable reason, was pointed in the direction of Pete Webster.

As Alex's hand reassured Billy, Pete stood next to her surveying the room with a bemused smirk. He was Billy's oldest and best friend. They went through high school as a pair of pranksters, closer than most brothers. After graduation Billy left for Syracuse and Pete left for the Army. He did a short stint in Vietnam. No one knew anything about it, but he returned a hard and bitter person, slowly finding comfort in a bottle or a doctor's prescription pad.

His trade, if you could call it that, was Private Investigator. He had a real knack for it, when he chose to work at it. Most of the time he just hung around the newspaper office running errands for Billy and getting into small bits of trouble. Tonight, he was parched and a bit hungry, amusing himself by scouting the room and laughing at the Boston Inteligencia and wondering what Billy saw in these people.

He spotted the bar, another stellar detective job, and decided to wander off in that direction. Turning towards Alex and Billy he politely asked if they, too, were sufficiently comfortable to indulge. They were not, so off he went.

"We should keep an eye on him, tonight. I don't like the look in his eye."

Alex followed Pete's progress across the crowded hall before answering Billy. "I know what you mean. These aren't, exactly, his favorite people."

"Let's just try to keep him from pontificating."

"God, yes! I'm not ready to pull his foot out of his mouth, tonight."

America's Front Page

As Billy watched Pete ease his way towards the bar, a tall unnaturally tanned and pony-tailed pair of sunglasses moved deftly about the room, heading in his direction. The moment Billy recognized his old nemesis the color drained from his face and tension stiffened his frame.

Blake Flatly, an old friend, himself a Syracuse grad, wandered about, glad-handing anyone who would so much as glance in his direction, in slowly shrinking circles towards the corner Billy and Fox had neatly staked out. Blake removed his glasses, as if announcing himself. He looked directly at Billy and smiled. A few quick steps and he was on him, no place for Billy to hide.

"Billy Petro, God, it's been a long time. I had a feeling that you'd be here! You still in the news game?" He reached out a hand that Billy barely shook. Alex edged her way in front of Billy, in her most protective mothering manner and introduced herself. While never having met this man before, she could tell by Billy's expression that this was not a scene about which he was overly enthused.

Respectfully, Blake shook her hand and made some pleasant remark about Billy being a lucky man, then; "Me, I've been so busy with my career that I've never had time to settle down. Now, I know why Billy left that two-bit gig in Buffalo." At that moment, Billy couldn't recall exactly why it was considered a bad thing to pop a lout in the mouth. He just knew that he wanted to, very badly. Of course, Pete was usually carrying a sidearm…

A smile crossed his face as he turned to Fox. "Blake, I'd like you to meet…"

"You don't have to introduce me to the Silver Fox." Blake almost pushed Alex to the floor, trying to proffer a hand to the esteemed Journalist. "I'm a big fan. I followed all your work at the Sun, Cuban Missile Crisis, the Cambodian bombings, all of it...great stuff!"

"That was a very long time ago. I've closed the book on that part of my life." Fox shook his hand and noticed it actually hurt a bit when he pulled it away. Billy added, "Blake, here, is a reporter on America's Front Page. You know the Television show that recreates news stories."

"Oh, yea. Sound bites and video flashes. Very interesting stuff."

"No offense, but it's the future. People don't have time to read every day, so we examine and present..."

"You condense and edit a story to show what you want people to see and how they should see it. Sounds a little like you don't trust people to have an actual thought process."

"It's what they want." Blake was a little defiant, but still respectful.

"It's what you give them. You should know the difference."

As Fox was about to expound on his problems with the industry as a whole and America's Front Page in particular, the small orchestra began a softly presented selection that signified the beginning of the program. Fox turned to Claire and for the first time in a while he was excited to deliver his little speech.

"Well, that's my signal, Mr. Flatly. It's been a pleasure."

"An honor, really, I mean that."

Fox walked away as Claire, holding his arm, gave Billy a little wink and a smile. Billy smiled back and watched Blake for a reaction. Blake was already looking around for someone else to try to impress.

"Cranky old bird, isn't he?"

"He's just proud of his profession, Blake. We could all learn a great deal from him."

"Yea, well, listen, it was good to see you're still alive. I understand you're working for Fox these days. You know I'm staying in your neck of the woods. Look me up some night and we can cop a buzz and talk about old times. I might even show you what I'm working on. Believe me, it's going to send plenty of Washington lifers packing."

"Well, I'm pretty busy…"

"I've got it, I'll swing by that rag of yours and we can swap horror stories."

"You do that."

Blake smiled at Alex and then patted Billy's shoulder before rushing off to find a seat next to someone important. Billy was wondering if he was working some story or actually having fun. Billy wondered if he knew the difference.

Alex could see the hollow look in Billy's eyes as he watched Blake disappear into the crowd. "You OK?"

"Sometimes, I just feel like I let myself down, that's all."

"He's a God awful guy, Bill. Don't let him get to you."

"It's not him. It's this whole room…this crowd."

Alex stared at him and rubbed his shoulder for a moment as Pete returned with a couple of drinks. He hands one to Billy. "Here, you look like you need it more than me."

"Billy just had a visit from Blake Flatly."

"That Cro-Magnon from Buffalo?"

"Let's not get into that, OK?"

The crowd was starting to settle down as Fox climbed the podium to begin his duties as

Toastmaster. He had written a glorious speech about Church and the important role of Journalism. Billy turned towards the dais, but his heart wasn't in it. Of course, he had read most of the speech and had helped smooth over some of the rough spots, but he didn't need to be reminded that he was not the reporter he wanted to be.

The Library

Sensing his uneasiness, Alex asked Billy if he wanted to get out of there and go home. He knew he couldn't do that, but he didn't want to stand around listening, either. Pete suggested they take a stroll through the library and all agreed it might be a good way to get Billy's mind off his inner demons for a short while.

The library had been built as a monument to JFK, the memories of Camelot, the legacy of his words. The first few rooms were structured to recreate his political triumphs, most notably a small theater to commemorate the Cuban Missile Crisis. Billy liked this part of the museum best. It brought him back to a time of good feelings and wonderment at all the possibilities the world held for him.

As a child, he was totally enthralled by the Kennedy years, following every story written and listening to his dad tell him stories about how he had met JFK in Everett during the Presidential campaign. He remembered it all, vividly.

Now, he would come to the museum to get some of those feelings back, to inspire him, to help him shed his general funk. Tonight was no exception. Wandering through the quiet corridors and examining the empty exhibit rooms brought a genuine sense of ease to him. They sat in one of the rooms that had been designed to emulate the White House Press Room and for a few short minutes they listened to Fox's speech being fed throughout the building over the sound system.

"...turbulent times, during which men like Warren Church, kept the nation informed, infused with passion and motivated to adhere to principals by which this unique institution, the fourth estate, contributes to the liberty and freedom of all Americans.

We owe this man a debt of gratitude that we can never repay. Honesty, integrity and, unlike me, brevity, are the hallmarks that will forever separate Warren Church from the ranks of simple editor to one of the most esteemed newsmen of our times. I give you the man we honor, here, tonight...Warren Church!"

A smattering of applause came across as Pete started to get up, bored with the speeches and wanting to see more of the exhibits.

Billy had wanted to hear more, but he acceded to Pete and they moved on into the only room where the memories were not glorious.

As they entered the hallway, with the many television screens showing various stages of the fateful news reports from that awful day, Billy got a shudder, as always. Most days he would simply walk through the room without stopping, but tonight they would have to look at the exhibit, because Pete had never before taken the time to come here.

They examined the multitudes of photographs, slowly remembering the dark, dreary time. They saw the motorcade, the confusion, the sadness on the face of Walter Cronkite. Pete read every caption, Billy and Alex just looking at the pictures. The final few photographs were the saddest; John John saluting his father, the unsaddled horse being pulled by the caisson.

"Thank you, my old friend. But, I think you have me confused with someone you know a bit better than me...yourself. At least, I hope that's the case because I thought I was listening to a eulogy. This is supposed to be a party, not a wake!"

Again, more laughter, as Pete stared at the famous "Tramps" photo, wondering why he didn't remember it from Billy's lectures on the assassination. "Well, I'll be damned. Hey,

Scoop, I don't remember them arresting anyone besides Oswald."

Billy walked over to the picture, put his arm on Pete's shoulder and shook his head. "You don't remember breakfast." They turned and walked towards the exit.

As they disappeared into the next room a tall older man appeared behind them. They hadn't noticed him following them through their little tour, watching their every movement.

Chapter Two

Everett Post Dispatch

Everett is a Blue Collar city of some 30,000 people that lies just beyond the Mystic River to the north of Boston. It is a small, crowded urban community of mostly two and three story homes passed within the family from generation to generation. Recently, however, a trend has left the city elders feeling a bit nervous about the future as much of the younger population has started to move away from the congestion, the noise and the brown hued skies that result from the power plant at the city's edge and those factories still in production.

Still, it was a mostly warm and friendly city, where way too many people knew your business and were ready to pass judgment or lend an opinion at the slightest encouragement. For a city not more than two square miles in scope there was an inordinate amount of Churches, corner convenience stores, funeral homes, liquor stores and pubs. Several recently scaled down industrial sites populated the outskirts of the city and, for years, provided the backbone of a healthy economy.

Now, some were mere shells of their former selves and some were just eyesores. Two or three remained robust and they were struggling. In the midst of all this economic uncertainty, there was a tension in the air that provided a new element to the routine that had been the essence of the city since the turn of the century.

Downtown was called the Square and was little more than a few banks, restaurants, small shops and hair salons all punctuating Broadway. Down a side street, off of the main drag, on a sleepy little corner stood a large wood-framed building with a stoop that was built right up against the curb. Glass windows covered two sides and a shiny new awning hung above them.

The gold lettering on the windows was old English and the brand new wooden sign over the door was neatly carved and painted. This was the home of the Everett Post Dispatch, the city's only daily paper for the last half century, now reduced to recording births, deaths, weddings and public service announcements. Billy knew that this was no place for a real reporter, but he had been there for over fifteen years.

He had sought refuge, there, after escaping his own little hell in Buffalo. The normalcy of the routine was a comfort to him and he relied on this to give him focus and meaning. While he kept toying with the idea that someday he would get back to serious writing, it never seemed realistic until Fox retired from Washington and bought the paper.

Now, Billy had renewed enthusiasm and had started to write a column of bits and pieces of gossip and short stories from around town. Last month he actually was able to put pressure on the local police to close a suspected crack house that had sprung up in one of the city's quieter neighborhoods. These last few days he was focusing his attention on the proposed sale of some city land to a questionable industrial development without any environmental studies or public hearings. For his efforts, he had had a personal visit from the mayor and several of the city's elite all trying to persuade him from continued rhetoric against the deal.

Claire was especially proud of the new "no parking" status the street had been given, making it awkward for advertisers to stop by and residents to come in and give Billy fodder for his column. Fox was amused by it all, knowing the sheer weight of his reputation protected Billy from any serious trouble. Still, he was mindful of the hazards and did his best to steer them clear of any minefields.

The morning was crisp and bright, a few light clouds dotting a perfect blue sky. There was a chill in the air as Billy unlocked the door and entered the front of the building. It was just after six thirty; Billy's usual check-in time. Since Fox had taken over he was finding that he was spending a lot more time in the office, by choice.

He walked past the deserted counter and the empty receptionist's desk to his own workstation, punching the startup button on his PC even before he took off his jacket and sat down. Once the screen declared him ready for work, he punched in a code and checked for any electronic mail. An old friend, now working at the Assessor's office was one of his prime sources of information on this land deal.

No mail, as yet. So he turned to his other interest; a story about times past when the city was alive and people spent their weekend nights in the Square, eating at restaurants and going to the Park Theater Movie House. An eternity, he thought, though in reality it was only thirty or forty years ago. No one was afraid to go out at night then; no gangs, no predators. Today, he would finish the first installment, of what, he hoped, would be a weekly feature.

The Post-Gazette's big edition was Saturday, as the paper did not publish on Sundays, leaving the market free for the big Sunday editions of the Boston papers. So Wednesday was the best day to prepare for the Saturday special features, when there were any, and the additional section dedicated to the upcoming week's church-related activities; the Bingo's, fund raisers, religious education classes and special functions. So far, it was a quiet Thursday morning.

By eight o'clock, the phone had rung just once, a wrong number. Billy was just about to put his story through the "Spell Check" when Fox and Claire arrived, laughing and feeling pretty good about Charlie's performance the night before. Billy stood and clasped Fox's hand, telling him how good the speech was before Claire raised an eyebrow and asked how he, Alex and Pete had managed to hear it. Billy, a pretty fast thinker, simply told her that all the festivities were broadcast over the PA and had interrupted their screening of the Cuban Missile Crisis exhibit.

Fox gratuitously accepted their good words and then decided it was time to turn his attention to the newspaper. He asked Billy what he had been up to. Billy told him he was catching up on his column. Fox, however, had another idea.

"Billy, how about writing a little article on that husband and wife who are going to run in the Boston Marathon next Monday. Living in Washington all these years, I forgot all about Patriot's Day except for when they mention the winner of the Marathon."

Clarie was taking off her coat. "You're right. I think it's such a nice idea, having a day off like that, after all it is the Revolution."

"I suppose it's like having Fat Tuesday off in New Orleans." Billy responded.

"Well, think about the story. I'd like to do something for Patriots Day. Maybe, check the files for some little known historical facts about the War. If I remember correctly, something happened around, here...some battle or something. Well, think about it."

As they chatted, an Everett Police cruiser pulled to a stop in front of the building. At the wheel was an old friend of Billy's, Sergeant Alton Chapp. He got out of the car; a tall muscular man in his forties, with flecks of white dotting his close cropped dark hair. The sergeant was one of only three minority officers on the police force, which greatly concerned him as the population of this once almost exclusively Irish and Italian city became more diversified.

He had risen to the rank of Sergeant in only five years on the force after ending a distinguished military career. Generally regarded as incorruptible, Billy relied on Al's information as unimpeachable. Only trouble was, Al was not a big talker.

He entered the office to find Billy at the counter to greet him. When he removed his sunglasses, Al looked as though he had just gone ten rounds with Mike Tyson. Billy started to ask him what was up, when Al interrupted.

"Just what were you and Pete up to last night?" an, obviously, exasperated Al wondered.

"Why…we were at that reception over at the JFK library. Is Pete in trouble, again?

"If he comes within a city block of my wife, he will be! He called me at four in the morning to tell me he couldn't remember where he left his car."

"Again?"

"He's got to stop bothering me, at home. Shiela's ready to freak out. She keeps asking if I can recommend a good shooter. And I'm not sure she's kidding, anymore!"

Billy laughs a little, shaking his head, as he walks to the window and sees Pete planted in the back seat of the cruiser, out like a light.

"I'm serious, man. Do something. Give him some work, anything. Some people just shouldn't have any time on their hands."

"Alright, Al. Let me check with Charlie. I'll take him home. By the way, where'd you find him?"

"He was wandering around Sacramone Park, throwing rocks at that old Peanutbutter plant."

Billy, laughing as he confers with Fox, grabs his coat and motions Al to the door. They walk outside to Al's car where Pete is sound asleep.

"Why don't I just follow you to Pete's."

Al gets in his car and revs up the engine waiting for Billy to pull along side. Once Billy arrives, Al pulls away from the curb and drives off to Pete's place. Off one of the main drags they pull down a side street of mostly two and three-decker homes, neatly trimmed and painted in quiet earthy tones. The homes are close together and the only trees, here, are planted along the sidewalks, old enough to offer some shade in the summer, but not big enough to cover anyone's tiny lawn.

Al pulls to a stop in front of a three family house and opens the back door. Pete is starting to wake up. Al grabs him under the arms, extracts him from the car and props him up against its side. Billy had driven past them, looking for a place to park. As with most side streets, there was parking on only one side and most of that was taken up by residents not able to fit their cars in their driveways.

Pete's apartment was a basement affair, entered by a side door that was too short for most people to enter completely upright. It was off the driveway side and as AL waited for Billy he became more disturbed when he saw Pete's car snugly sitting in the drive, not ten paces from his door.

Billy walked to the car and snatched Pete, as Al was about to let him slide to the ground.

"I mean it, Billy, straighten his ass out. Look where he left it?"

"Come on, Al. Do you really want him driving like this?"

"Don't go there, man."

The two men walked Pete towards his doorway, Pete offering little assistance. As they approached, the mobile communications unit in Al's car summons him. They prop Pete against the house as Al runs back to the car. Sticking his head inside, he answers the call. All Billy can hear is static.

Al lifts his head out of the car and yells over to Billy; "You're on your own. We've got a hit and run at the corner of Walnut and Hancock. Get him settled and I'll catch you up at the scene."

Billy nods his head and as Al pulls away he tries to muscle Pete towards the apartment. When they do reach the door, it is unlocked, as always, Pete believing his security tag on the window will keep away the punk burglars, the only ones he feared.

Once inside, they moved to the couch where Pete collapsed in a heap, half unconscious. He was mumbling, but Billy couldn't make out any of the words. The apartment was bare like most non-essential aspects of Pete's life. There was the large couch, a coffee table and a couple of big comfortable chairs. The kitchen was little more than a sink, refrigerator, stove and surrounding counter. Pete liked things as simple as possible. There was an almost empty bedroom; the couch opening to a bed, when Pete took the time and effort to set it up.

Billy walked into the kitchen, noticed the Police Radio and turned it on, mostly static, interrupted by police blatherings about the accident and who should be sent to do whatever needed to be done. He poured a glass of water and grabbed a couple of aspirins from the cupboard above the sink.

Satisfied that a minor disaster had been avoided, he walked back to Pete and put the glass and pills on the top of the coffee table. He told Pete to be a good boy and stay put until Alex could get there. Pete mumbled back as Billy got to the door and left. Once the door closed, Pete sat up, as if teetering on the edge of a cliff and shook his head. He picked up the glass of water and stared at it, as if he hadn't seen one in a long time.

Shaking his head in recognition he got up and trudged to the sink, where he poured out the contents of the glass. Fishing through one of the lower cabinets, he found a fifth of Bourbon. He poured two fingers worth into the glass and proceeded to wash down the aspirins with two long gulps of his favorite elixir.

Waverly and Hancock

Billy arrived at the intersection of Waverly and Hancock streets to find a buzz of activity. Al was standing at the foot of the stairs leading to a two family house next door to the apartment building that was situated at the corner. He was talking with an older Black woman who was very animated. At the corner of the street was a traffic light, which she explained was red when a small dark blue car cruised to a stop, just behind an old run down Street Cleaner.

As the driver waited for the light to change, a small boy came running out of the driveway across from her house and smacked right into the rear side of the car. The boy bounced off of the car and into the street, sitting and crying as the driver of the car eased his way around the Street Cleaner and sped away, down Hancock heading towards Malden, another blue-collar city located just to the north.

Billy took a few notes as three policemen scoured the sidewalks and gathered what ever they could that might help identify the car. The young boy was seated on the rear bumper of a city ambulance getting first aid from an EMT. He appeared to be fine except for a scraped knee and small bump on his head.

The woman on the porch, Mrs. Burke, gave Al a first-rate description of the car and the last letters on the plate. Seeing Billy, Al used the opportunity to get away from Mrs. Burke, a notorious town crier who had made Al's life a living hell on several occasions in the past.

"I don't get it." started Al. "The kid literally ran into him, he was stopped. Now tell me why he would take off…why?"

"To keep your life interesting?"

"I don't know, but it doesn't make any sense. Now, I gotta track him down and do all sorts of paperwork that, quite frankly, I shouldn't have to do." Al shook his head and, "I'm not a happy man, Bill." He turned around and went back to the street, looking for clues. Billy walked over to Mrs. Burke and asked if she had had any ideas why the man would just take off without, at least, confirming that the child was okay.

"Now, how am I supposed to know that? You want me to do your work for you, too! I'm already doin' the cops' work."

"What an interesting old character." Billy thought to himself. As he was about to ask her if she could remember anything about the driver that might help find him, Al came up behind him and cleared his throat.

"I already got her statement. Do yourself a favor and keep it short. She'll wear you out."

As he was talking one of the younger policemen came running over.

"Sarge, we got a hostage situation over at the Hospitality Inn. Captain says to get right over there. He says he'll meet your there with a SWAT team."

"A SWAT team! We don't have a SWAT team! Goddamn it, all Hell has to break loose at the same time. Tell Roselli I'm on my way." Then turning to Billy; "I'll meet you over there. Take my advice, don't ask the woman another question or you'll be here all day."

A patrol car raced by, sirens blaring, lights flashing, as Al made a mad dash to his car across the street. Suddenly, the buzz of police activity was gone and Billy found himself alone with Mrs. Burke. She just stared at him defiantly and he decided that Al was right.

Hospitality Inn

The Hospitality Inn was an eight-story structure located at the edge of the city, an older hotel that had been there for generations of

Proms, Rotary Luncheons and Weddings. It had the only truly four star restaurant in the city and it was the kind of place where people went for a nice dinner before a movie or just a well-earned night out. The bar had a friendly neighborhood feel where weekend regulars would come in to watch a ballgame or share another week's worth of same old, same old.

The hotel, itself, was decent. It catered to small conferences and was the kind of place you would book visiting relatives or business travelers not looking to pad an expense account. The business was steady through almost any economic time and most of the employees were long-term locals.

When Billy arrived the lobby was full of policemen suiting up in black bulletproof vests and helmets. A communications center was set up behind the large wooden check-in counter. Walkie-talkies were being handed out and Al was giving instructions to three or four men who fanned out in various directions around the property.

A tall gray-haired man wearing a dark suit that hung loosely about his large frame approached Al from behind the counter. He was holding a walkie-talkie and speaking to the first patrolman who arrived on the scene. The patrolman was outside the laundry room on the third floor where, it was believed, the perp had taken a maid hostage.

"Sergeant, are we ready? Holden is getting nervous up there." Captain Roselli was a twenty-year veteran of the force after a stellar career in the military that included tours of duty in both Korea and Vietnam, the last conflict earning him two commendations and a lifetime of bad memories.

"We're set. I sent out three snipers, they should be in place, just in case he gets by us."

"Then let's get moving, I want this over and done with as quick as possible." Roselli went back to the counter and took off his jacket. Al motioned to Billy who moved over to him for some information.

"We've got one guy up on the third floor. The house dick found him breaking into one of the rooms on the fourth floor and chased him down to the third where he grabbed one of the maids and pulled her into the laundry room."

Billy knew they would be moving quickly so he asked just one quick question; "Who's room?"

"Some reporter from out of town, as far as I can tell. Right now that's not important." Al saw Roselli motion him and they were off with four or five patrolmen up the stairs and, shortly, out of sight.

Billy walked over to the desk, wanting to get more information on the occupant of the room in question, when he saw Blake enter the Hotel. Billy shook his head. It figured, he thought, that the biggest story he's had to cover since he took this job, centered around his old nemesis.

Blake did not see Billy and didn't seem too concerned with all the commotion. Before Billy could get to him, he was intercepted by Pete, still shaky, but surprisingly coherent.

"What are you doing here? Shouldn't you be sleeping this off?" Billy was incredulous.

"And miss all this excitement! Are you serious?" He studied Billy who gave him his best disapproving look. "So, what's up, Scoop?"

"Some guy is holed up in the laundry room up on the third floor with one of the housekeepers."

"Perfect. You want to get in on the action?" Pete asked.

"And, just exactly how are we going to do that?"

"Simple, I used to be the House dick, remember? We can go downstairs to the central laundry. All those other rooms have chutes that lead down stairs. Let's go!"

Billy never had gotten used to Pete's seat of the pants way of doing things, but he always trusted him and Pete had never done anything to discourage that trust. He figured at the very least, it was better than hanging around the lobby waiting for them to come down with the perp.

As they were headed for the stairs that led to the garage and from there the laundry facility, Blake spotted them and followed. Billy grabbed Pete by the arm when Blake came up behind them.

"Well, Billy boy, I thought this was supposed to be some sleepy little urban oasis, what gives?" Blake feigned interest.

"We got a hostage situation up stairs, we're going down to the laundry to see if we can get some perspective." Billy couldn't make up his mind if he wanted Blake around or not, but it was no longer up to him.

"The laundry?"

"Just come along, I'll explain later."

They moved down the stairs and through the garage to the back entrance of the laundry. It was a large open room with bins of soiled linens and long racks where the clean sheets and towels were piled. There was a truck bay, where the old washing machines used to be. Now, there was just one machine and a dryer for emergencies, all the other cleaning being outsourced to save money.

In the middle of the room was a long cylindrical metal tube that came from the upper floors and emptied into a bin beneath the large mouth opening at the bottom. Pete quickly removed the bin and peered up into the chute. Half of his body disappeared from view.

Above him, all the small doorways were closed. Some muffled sounds could be heard but he could not place them. Billy tapped him on the leg and asked if he could see or hear anything. Blake just stood back and watched from the doorway.

On the third floor, Al knelt along the corridor wall outside the door to the laundry. Roselli talked into a walkie-talkie and then motioned Al to resume talking. Al had been on the force for twenty years and this was his first experience with a hostage situation. In fact, no one on the force had any such experience. While the small city had many of the same problems any big city had, there were few incidents like this.

Oh, there were the house break-ins, store holdups, the occasional bar fight or brawl among youth gangs, but there hadn't been a murder or high profile crime since the late sixties when someone car bombed a local attorney who didn't do a very good job of defending an organized crime figure. Today, they were forced to, mostly, improvise. Al took the lead and approached the door with reassuring tones about what he commanded outside the door and how there could be no escape.

There was only silence from inside, save the occasional whimper from the poor maid who was caught in a situation beyond the scope of her limited imagination. Al tried attempt after attempt to engage the unknown assailant in some form of meaningful dialog, but the man remained silent.

There was an edgy atmosphere in the corridor, Roselli fearing that he was about to lose his grip on the frustrated patrolmen all around him. He had been concerned from the beginning that they would not be equipped to handle such a crisis. Because of that, he had called the Staties and they had promised to be there within the hour. That time was fast approaching and he still hoped to have everything resolved before they arrived.

In the basement, Billy and Blake had taken seats on some of the stacks of laundry strewn about the room. Pete continued to stare into the chute. He leaned down and looked at Billy.

"You know, I could shimmy my way up this thing and surprise the son-of-a-bitch. What do you think?"

Billy looked at him and just shook his head. "Let the police handle this, will you please."

"You got no sense of adventure." was Pete's only reply.

Then Blake piped in; "How long do you propose to just sit here? This is not what a reporter does. He goes after the story. Imagine if you could get in there to ask him some questions before the police came in and took him out."

"Don't be melodramatic. That's movie stuff. Not the real world." Billy said it without an ounce of conviction, because as much as he hated to admit, he felt that Blake was in a better position to know about these things. After all hadn't he done that story last year about the hostage taking at Angel Notch in Utah? In fact, Blake had gotten an interview with the leader of the White Supremacists the day before their eventual surrender.

He took a lot of heat for sneaking his way in and out without being detected by the FBI. There was even speculation that he had faked the interview, but no proof to make an absolute determination either way. Billy believed he had pulled it off.

While Billy sat there speculating on what to do, his mind was made up for him. A soft metallic noise came from inside the chute. Pete looked up and motioned Billy over. They looked up and saw that, now, one of the doors was open. It was the third floor.

Pete stepped out from under the chute and told Billy and Blake to step back. He grabbed one of the laundry sacks and crouched down a few steps away. Then they heard the sound of a man trying to shimmy down the chute, shoes clanging against the sides, slipping as he descended.

They all saw the shoes as they appeared, followed by legs and, finally, the lower torso. Pete was on him in a flash, first throwing the sack of laundry to take out his legs, then rushing to subdue him as he bounced off the side of the chute and fell to the floor. The two struggled on the floor for a couple of moments, but Pete had the upper hand, easily controlling the older man, using a chord from one of the laundry bags to bind his hands behind him.

Billy and Blake emerged from hiding as Pete pushed Hoffman Muir against a laundry basket and called up to the officers above. Billy heard voices and then, looking into the chute, saw Al poke his head out into the darkness.

Within minutes Al, Roselli and three uniforms were in the laundry room taking control of Muir. They began to frisk him.

"Don't bother, he hasn't any ID. I checked." Pete was still winded, leaning against the chute, flexing his right arm.

"Looks a little old for a cat burglar, don't you think?" Asked Blake. Al looked at him, puzzled.

"You that reporter, fellow, Billy told me about?"

"I guess."

Roselli had tried to ask Muir several questions, but he didn't voice a single response. Frustrated, Roselli, ordered his men to take him to the station house and then turned his rage on Pete.

"What the hell did you think you were doing down here?!?"

"Your job?"

Roselli was in his face, chest-to-chest, eye to eye. Pete was emotionless but sturdy, not wanting to appear to back down. He almost wanted to laugh, but knowing that Roselli was not a man to get riled, he tried to remain calm.

Roselli

Pete's feud with Roselli was an old one. They had seemed to be in each other's way ever since Roselli came to town. There was no underlying reason, no run-ins, just an honest dislike between them. It had erupted, on a small scale, once or twice, but never anything physical or permanent.

Roselli tried to pull Pete's license on several occasions, most often after Pete had drunk himself into doing something stupid, like papering the Mayor's house or brawling at one of the local pubs. In fact, he had Pete barred from most of them, but Everett being a blue collar town had many small taverns and pubs. More than Roselli could control. Pete had a lot of friends in this city and always paid for the damage and never seriously injured anyone.

Only once was Roselli able to get Pete's license pulled for a couple of months after he, foolishly advised a client not to cooperate with an investigation. But, Pete gained a reputation for bucking the system and became a popular figure with an expanding clientele of downtrodden, set-upon citizens and minor league hoods.

Of course, Pete and prosperity are not part of the same equation, so he did whatever it took to stifle his own success and remain at odds with the most powerful man in the Department.

"Sergeant, I want all of these clowns down at the station for questioning." He backed away and stormed out the door. Muir had been removed and when Al, strongly advised that they cooperate Blake laughed, informing Al that there was no way to compel him to say a word about what had happened.

"I hope you won't get offended, but you can ask all you want…I'm not going anywhere. I was just along for the laughs."

"Well, what if I told you it was your room he was breaking into when he got caught. You interested, now?"

"Come on, Blake. Let's just see what's what." Billy was getting more curious and a bit jealous, at the same time. Now, Pete was amused.

Chapter Three

The Story

Billy, Blake and Pete sat in one of the more uncomfortable waiting areas in the newly built Police Headquarters. It was a modest three story brick building built by the taxpayers after a contentious election four years ago. With the backing of the Police Union and some hard lobbying by some of the veteran officers, the citizenry had decided that a new building was needed to replace the decaying turn of the century edifice that blocked the last piece of major development in the middle of Everett Square.

The new building was built on the outskirts of town, next to the old Hockey Rink and the even older Recreation Center. There were plenty of homes around it, as was the case in every corner of the crowded city, but it was off the beaten track and out of sight for the majority of it's citizens.

Thoroughly modern, in every respect, it housed every convenience a politician could show off to the public. Roselli's office was a large glass enclosure on the second floor, at the end of a large area of small cubicles used by the four full time detectives and some of the more senior on-duty officers. Two small cushioned benches were stuck against a wall across from the bank of windows overlooking the recreation venues to the north.

The blinds were pulled up and Billy stared out at the budding Spring foliage on the few trees lining Elm Street. Pete had gotten restless and walked over to the water cooler, pouring himself a drink, taking it down in one long gulp. Blake just stared at Roselli's office, waiting to voice his extreme displeasure with the treatment being accorded one of America's most recognizable tabloid reporters.

They had been waiting for almost an hour when the door opened and Al appeared. He scurried past them to a set of stairs at the opposite end of the room. Two detectives, who had had their heads buried in paperwork got up to peer at Al over the cubicle walls. They spoke to each other in hushed tones, and then, laughed.

Billy started to go after Al when Roselli appeared at his door and called out to Billy and Blake, telling Pete to "stay put" for a few more minutes. Billy took a long look at the stairs as Al disappeared. Then he looked at Blake and, the two of them, walked into the Captain's office.

The office was cold, sterile. There were no pictures on the two-side walls and with windows making up the back and front walls, there was an uneasy openness to the space. There were two lateral file cabinets along one wall, above which was hung a framed citation for duty above and beyond. The opposite wall was blank with a small credenza nestled against it. Three large stacks of unkempt files were splayed across the surface, completely covering a set of desk encyclopedias and old box of cigars.

The desk was clean, blotter in place, phone and intercom unit neatly positioned to Roselli's right hand opposite a small clock and one small picture frame of Roselli's young son and deceased wife. His chair was backed up to the rear window which overlooked the building's parking lot and the, equally new, Central Fire Station.

Billy and Blake sat on the two chairs opposite Roselli's desk. Roselli had moved to the window, where he stood with his back to them, standing, staring at some unknown target. Billy made special note of the coat rack, neatly placed in the corner, from which hung Roselli's sports jacket and holster. He didn't really expect any fireworks, but with Roselli, you just never knew.

Blake had had enough. He stood. "Just how long do you intend this little power play to go on? I've had enough! Now, what in the hell are you trying to do, here!?!"

Billy knew that wasn't a good idea and as Roselli slowly turned around he had a sudden impulse to duck and cover. Roselli stared at

Blake, but didn't, immediately, say a word. Just a hard burning stare.

Blake sat, having seen that unreasoning stare before and knowing there would be a better time to challenge him. Roselli, eyes still fixed on Blake, sat as well.

"What you are doing here is helping me solve a riddle. You like riddles Mr. Flatly?"

"Not particularly."

"Well, I've got a hell of a problem and you seem to be right in the middle of it. Mind telling me why some two bit hood would be trying to break into your room?"

"I'm sure I don't know."

"You're not working some story, you feel compelled to share with me?"

"I'm here on vacation. I came to see my old friend, here."

"That true Bill?"

"Don't let me get in the way, I'm enjoying the show."

Roselli got out of his seat and leaned on the front of the desk.

"Cut the bullshit, both of you. We don't have this kind of crime in Everett and I won't stand for it. Now, I'll ask you one more time, what the hell was he looking for?"

"I don't know and if I did, I wouldn't tell you. You know what I do for a living…sometimes I piss people off. Right now, I'm a bit pissed, myself. You haven't let me get back to my room to see if anything's missing. You know he could simply be a thief…you have that kind of crime, here, don't you?"

Billy had been waiting for a classic Roselli tirade, but none was forthcoming. That puzzled him.

"What's up Cap'? Who is this guy?"

Roselli went back to his seat.

"I don't know. He never said a word. Just made his phone call, long distance, mind you, and ten minutes later we had to release him. But I think your friend knows."

"I'm serious. I don't know who he is." Blake stared at Roselli as he answered, starting to think that it would be a good idea to find out whom this guy was.

"What story are you working on? I hear things."

Billy was growing uneasy, not being a part of the conversation both of them shadow boxing, leaving him to referee. That was not his style.

"What kind of things?" Billy had tried to show that he wasn't at all concerned with Blake's story, but now that Muir had been released without, even giving them a name, he couldn't help but be interested.

"I got friends over in Chelsea say that he's been spotted at the docks, late at night, just sitting in his car."

Blake stared beyond, Roselli, trying not to listen too intently. He was getting curious, but he didn't want Roselli to know that.

"Also, it appears that we're going to have some visitors in a couple of days. There are three additional reservations for rooms under Flatly's name, starting day after tomorrow. A camera crew, maybe?"

"Enough! I'm not going to tell you squat about my story and there isn't a damn thing you can do to force me to. I'm a reporter. I make enemies. I don't know this perp or who he's working for. Now, unless you intend to charge me with something, I'm going to walk out of here."

Blake got up and started to move towards the door. Roselli stood, but made no move to stop him.

"You coming, Petro?"

"I'll be right there."

"Suit yourself."

Blake reached the door and then turned to Roselli.

"I'm not trying to make enemies here, but I don't like these games, Captain." With that he exited into the waiting area. Through the window, Roselli could see Blake walk over to Pete and start an animated conversation.

"I don't like the looks of that."

"Listen, Cap, what's this all about? Who let him go?"

"I wish I knew. But, you can be damn sure, I'm going to find out!"

Roselli continued to watch Blake and Pete talk together.

"Why do you continue to hang around with that lowlife?"

"Pete's no lowlife. He's had some bad breaks. He's never been able to let some things go."

"He's always been trouble. I don't trust him. You know I'd pull his license if I had just cause."

"You gonna try to do that now?"

"Nah, but I'm gonna rattle his cage a little." Roselli smiled for the first time.

"Give him a break, will you?"

"Not a chance! I've got to have some fun in this job. Tell him to come in when you leave. By the way, that guy Blake is trouble, steer clear of him if you can."

"Don't think I can, Cap, I'm a reporter and right now he might be my story."

From the waiting area, Pete was watching Billy as he got up and moved to the door. Blake was going on about Roselli and Pete was trying to appear disinterested, all the while making mental notes of his inflamed speech.

The Morning Edition

Back at the paper, Fox was putting together the bits and pieces of what Billy had told him, regarding the accident, into a cohesive story.

Every now and then he still liked to try his hand at writing, though he didn't want to do Billy's job.

Claire was sitting at the workstation next to him, putting the final touches on the morning edition. She and Fox were enjoying their semi-retirement. When they were in Washington she had little opportunity to assist in putting the paper together. Now, she was a part of the daily grind, compiling the everyday features and helping to put together advertising copy for the regular customers brought in by the one man sales staff, a retired city employee needing to pick up a little extra cash.

Advertising was not the strength of the paper, new revenue only coming at the expense of replacing a closing business in this aging town. Even though, after careful analysis of their balance sheets showed a mere break even position, they were enjoying their attempts to keep the paper from becoming a dried up weekly, that was little more than a rag for announcing births, deaths, engagements and retirements.

As Fox worked on his story she watched him out of the corner of her eye. She had been with Fox a long time and still reveled in watching the joy on his face whenever he was actually writing. He hadn't been a regular reporter in over thirty years, ascending to an Editor's post during the Johnson administration. Claire was hired as his

Administrative Assistant shortly thereafter and had been with him ever since.

Looking back, she was never able to pinpoint exactly when it became more than a working relationship, but she remembered that a gradual understanding had developed between them. Now, they had found an ideal situation to enjoy their time together. With Billy, there, Fox only had to work when he wanted and could devote his considerable energies to causes close to his heart. One of his favorite causes was trying to convince Billy to resume his career after foundering in Everett, reliving a death for which he blamed himself and his profession.

Now, with a small buzz of activity, Claire could sense that old drama unfolding. Urgency replacing the mundane. Passion replacing complacency.

Billy checked in with Fox, bringing a story on the break-in already on tape and a police snapshot of the still unidentified Hoffman Muir.

"Let's get that on the front page right next to the accident story. I've got that ready to go. Let Claire transcribe your notes. You can proof this for me."

Billy dropped a small handheld tape recorder on Claire's workstation and sat next to Fox. They went over the story as Claire started transcribing.

In the midst of all the activity the phone rang. It was Al. A man had come into the station claiming to be the driver of the car that had struck the child. They had given him a Desk Appearance ticket and let him go.

Billy asked him if Pete was still there and when Al said he was just finishing up with Roselli, Billy asked if he could give the details to Pete and have him rush them over to the paper. Al said he would send along a picture of the driver. Billy thanked him and got back to work.

The sun was going down by the time Pete arrived, fresh from his renewed scuffle with Roselli. He placed the picture on the desk where Billy and Fox were working and asked Claire how long she thought they would be working. She was excited to tell him that they would be there well into the night.

Normally, a late night at the Gazette was six o'clock, but tonight it would be much later. After a short discussion Pete was volunteered for food duty, being sent out to pick up Chinese for the crew.

It was close to midnight when Billy finally got home to his sixth floor Condo just off the Square. He felt good, a gentle buzz of adrenaline flowing through his body. Billy put down his notes and brewed himself a small two-cup pot of coffee. There was a cool April breeze, but Billy wanted to sit on his balcony and stare at the Boston cityscape only a couple of miles across the Mystic River.

He bundled himself in a winter jacket, grabbed a folding chair from the closet and sat outside, his feet resting on the bottom railing. He watched the planes above the city and drifted off into a restless haunting sleep.

He met Terry when the two of them were in the eighth grade, immediately becoming enamored by her charms and astounded by the easy way she was able to mingle with any group. By the time they made it to the ninth grade they were inseparable. They became each other's life. All through high school they shared their entire worlds, their deepest thoughts, most intimate moods.

There was a slight bump in the road when Billy won a scholarship to Syracuse to develop his skills as a Journalist. Terry went on to UMass, Amherst to study the human mind. They saw each other, almost every weekend, the long drive getting shorter and shorter as each year passed. By the time they were seniors, they were taking time off to spend entire weeks together, planning their lives and enjoying the last days of pure irresponsible fun.

In the late Fall Billy got an assignment as an intern at a Buffalo daily, soon becoming a regular employee and upon graduation, a starting assignment in the Obit section. Terry took an extra semester to finish and upon completing her coursework, she moved to Buffalo. There she entered a graduate program at the University and, soon, started her career as a counselor at a local Homeless shelter.

For the next three years life was a series of wonderous experiences for the charmed couple. They set up house and made plans to marry once both had more firmly established themselves. As Billy's career went into orbit they got closer and closer to setting a date. But there were some insecure moments for Terry. Sometimes, late at night, with Billy out covering some story, she would sit in the dark and wonder if they could hold their relationship together if he became as prominent a figure as they had fantasized.

From time to time she would express her doubts and he would reassure her as if she were a silly child searching for her parent's approval. Eventually, they set their sites on a date, well beyond the life expectancy of Billy's current City Hall corruption story. But the date would never come and Billy found himself following her body home, determined never to leave her again.

On the balcony, all of his old demons emerged; blame and regret merging into a single horrible gutwrenching feeling that dominated most of his private moments. Pete and Alex kept him sane, but he still harbored a pain that was too deep to ever be expunged. One that would emerge all too often, whenever he found himself alone or with time on his bloodstained hands.

Billy was nearly alone, now, both of his parents having died; his dad two years ago, his mom just before last Christmas. His only sibling, a sister, went to school in Arizona and never moved back to Boston. She was married and secure, entertaining Billy once a year, during his summer vacation, in her sprawling ranch home in the Valley of the Sun. A more different world, he could not imagine.

At times, he would sit alone in the dark and try to imagine where he would be, today, had things gone differently. The more time passed, the harder it became to imagine he would be anywhere else. As he sat there, at least tonight, he could picture a very different world, one with excitement, poignancy and purpose. Tonight, finally, he felt like a reporter, again. It had been a long time.

He awoke from his restless sleep, his mind too active to really fall into that deep, restful, peaceful sleep into which he sought refuge on most nights. So, he stared out at the perfect skyline and noticed a nearly full moon illuminating the skyscrapers of the darkened city.

It got a bit too breezy to stay on the balcony, so around one, he went inside. He put the tube on and watched some innocuous Talk Show for a few minutes. Nothing there to calm his mind. He thought of pouring himself a drink, but he had been that route and it never cured his insomnia. He needed something to calm himself down, stop the racing mind and leave himself with some semblance of mental acuity in the morning.

Around the corner and a block from the Square there was a twenty four hour pharmacy. He grabbed his coat and wallet, took the elevator to the lobby and upon exiting bumped into Blake, standing there, eyeing the mailboxes, looking for Billy's apartment number. Billy approached apprehensively, not certain that this was the best way to deal with insomnia.

"To what do I owe this pleasure?" Billy startled him.

"What?...well, great! I guess I don't have to worry about disturbing you. Where are you off too?"

"I was headed to the Drug store for something to help me get to sleep, but, maybe, you'll do."

"That hurts, man. I want to catch up with an old bud, what's wrong with that? You've been dissing me since I got, here." Blake was on the defensive.

"You've been strutting since you got, here." Billy replied without pausing to consider Blake's charge.

"Well...maybe, you've got a point. You want to go get a bite, somewhere, I haven't eaten since breakfast."

"I suppose. There's a diner down on the Parkway that's open all night." Billy knew Meehan's Truck Stop all too well. It was the only restaurant in the city with table service after midnight. Fast food places just never seemed to do the trick.

Blake, his rental parked at the hydrant in front of the building, pulled away from the curb screeching his tires. They arrived at the diner in less than ten minutes during which time they exchanged pleasantries and avoided any talk of the day's events. Once seated inside, Blake told Billy he wanted to compare notes...that he believed they were working on the same story.

"And how did you arrive at that conclusion?" Billy asked.

"Obviously, the perp was trying to get into my room and it wasn't a simple B and E."

"Do you know what he was after?"

"Specifically, no, but I'm working on a real blockbuster." He lowered his voice and looked around.

The diner was busier than he thought it would be at one thirty in the morning. There were four or five truckers sitting at the counter and several booths were occupied by couples or groups that appeared to be local gangbangers. The diner was right on the Parkway, a neon lighted strip of gas stations, repair shops, lumberyards, discount stores, storage facilities and the occasional fast food franchise. It was a truck route that separated Everett and Chelsea and as such, was busy all night long with drivers whose cargo was either headed to or from Logan Airport located just beyond the Chelsea waterfront.

Blake glanced around and once certain that no one was concerned with their presence he leaned forward and related his tale to Billy.

A Hint of Scandal

Last September I was in Chicago for some press luncheon when I was approached by an old friend. He was working for the county coroner and had come across a pair of unrelated but similar deaths. Both victims had died from a rare tropical disease. When he ran it through the computer, he found that they were the only two deaths from that disease that they had on file.

It didn't make me particularly interested until he told me that one of them was a low level hood who had been connected to a guy named Sonny Fitzgerald. I knew him from a story on the Chicago mob wars a few years back. No one in that mob moved without Sonny's okay. I figured, what the hell, let me see what this other guy was doing and how the two might be connected.

The other stiff was a US representative to the OAS. It put me to thinking and I backtracked both of them over the previous six months and, wouldn't you know it, they had both been to New Orleans and Miami at the same times.

I wasn't working on anything at the time so I got permission to do a prelim workup and see if there was anything there. I went down to New Orleans and found out our OAS rep had an interest in a warehouse out on the Mississippi River. I visited the place and it was pretty run down. I checked the ownership through four layers of dummy corporations to an SG Enterprises.

Then I went to Miami and traced both of them to a place called Steamboat Key. It's a little spit of a place, an inn, some small retail shops and a fisherman's paradise. The biggest business is a Hydroplane sightseeing tour company, simply called Tour Services, which has four planes and twice as many employees as it needs to run the place. They control half the marina.

I traced their ownership through a few layers of paper and came across the same company that owns the warehouse in New Orleans. Bingo! There's something rotten in Denmark.

I had a friend of mine, one of the producers from the show, look into SG Enterprises and she tells me they're a paper entity with some strange connections to Government agencies. Now, I start to sniff around Steamboat Key and sit down with some old guy who harvests Conch shells for a living. He tells me that over the last year or so the place has begun to hop for the first time since the CIA was training Cubans before the operation was shut down after the Bay of Pigs.

I'm thinkin' government and I'm smellin' organized crime. This guy tells me that the planes go out at night and intercept small craft just beyond the outer reef. He says he can see it from his shack. So I stay with him that night and the next. The second night I wake up to the sound of one of the planes at about two in the morning.

I went down to the shore with an infrared camera and took some shots of them loading something from the planes onto the boats and then takin' something from the boats and loading it onto the plane. They were putting long cylindrical boxes on the boats and taking off large canvas boxes that looked a lot like marijuana bales.

The next day there is a buzz of activity with several trucks moving in and out of the seaplane base from around eight or nine in the morning til noon. After that, things calmed down and the place was dead again. Until, later that afternoon, when I spotted a couple of State Police cars parked down at the shore foraging through overgrown mangroves and pulling something from the shallow water. It was the body of some gray-haired man with tattoos all over his upper body.

I spoke with one of the troopers and he said it looked like a hit. He also said that the body was placed where it would be easily found and that no identifying aspects of the body had been disturbed. I became curious. He was a retired professor whose name was Gene Hayes, age 72, retired for around ten years.

On my way out of South Florida I stopped by the campus and asked a few questions about our murder victim and found that there were rumors that he once worked out of the University on the JMWave project which had something to do with monitoring the activities of Cuban exiles in South Florida during the early 1960's. I thought the whole thing was strange, but I wasn't certain there was any connection to the seaplanes or the activity I saw out on the water.

I went back to my home base in DC where I got a hold of two more interesting pieces of information. First, the company owned other properties, including the place over in Chelsea that I've been watching. And secondly, that our Mr. Hayes had, at one time, been a recruiter for the CIA. I still got someone digging into this guy's background.

At that point, I took a short assignment and let this thing sit for a time, while I tried to put it into some sort of usable context. Then, earlier this month, there was another coincidence. A man named Fernando Cabrerra was found murdered in a warehouse on the docks in New Orleans, the same warehouse owned by this shadow company. So naturally, I picked up the story and came up here to see what was doing at the Bonner Fishing Company, the only operating business on their list of properties, aside from the seaplane tours.

He finished his story and glanced around over his shoulder at the thinning crowd. It was now almost three o'clock. He turned back to Billy, looking for some reaction, but Billy continued to stare straight ahead.

"What do you know about this Cabrerra guy?" Billy was trying to connect all the pieces on his own.

"Nothing, yet. I didn't go down to New Orleans because I've been there and it's a very quiet town for outsiders."

Billy noticed the check on the table for the first time and threw a fivespot down, then rose and with Blake by his side left the diner and went out into the cool dark night. Blake drove them back to Billy's place where he pulled to a stop and looked into Billy's eyes.

"One more thing. The dude who died in Chicago, the hood, he was tied to an armory theft at a base outside Chicago. They got guns, ammo...some pretty sophisticated stuff."

"Did you tell anyone else about this?" Billy was wondering why Blake had left out that key point?

"No. None of it."

"We'll talk again, tomorrow."

"I know I can trust you, but let's keep this between us for right now."

Billy got out of the car just before Blake peeled away from the curb. He watched him, disappear into the night, then turned and walked upstairs to his condo knowing that getting to sleep wouldn't be easy.

Chapter Four

Mrs. Burke

Billy hadn't slept very well when the alarm went off at six. He decided that he couldn't do his job without some semblance of rest, so he rolled over and went back to sleep. By the time he awoke it was past eight and as was usually the case when he varied from his normal habit, he was fogbound and cotton-mouthed.

He rolled out of bed and grabbed the phone, calling Fox to let him know that he would be late, but that he had some insight into what might be going on. While he went about his morning business, he fought with himself over whether or not he could tell Fox some or all of what he and Blake had discussed. They were no more than old colleagues, not friends, but he always prided himself on being trustworthy.

He hurried himself around the apartment and by quarter to nine was ready to get to the office and had decided to tell Fox a few of the bare essentials, what he thought might relate to his story. Of course, once out on the street, fresh air clearing the cobwebs away as he walked to the paper, he wasn't quite sure what was and what was not related. In theory, the break-in must be tied to the whole set of events that Blake was trailing. In fact, unless he knew exactly what the thief was after, none of it was specific enough to be useful. More digging, he concluded and no one he had ever met was better at digging than Fox.

By the time he reached the office he had run Blake's story around so many times that he was convinced that what Blake had seen was a simple transfer of guns for drugs and that some very shadowy, most likely powerful entities were involved. The murders of the two old men were probably related, but how was not clear.

He reached the office a little after nine walking quickly into the building anxious to sit down with Fox and get his feedback. Closing the door behind him, he noticed Fox and Claire at the counter, talking to Mrs. Burke, the woman who had witnessed the hit and run. She was loudly protesting some part of the story, telling Fox that they had got it all wrong. Billy was sorry that he had been late.

"You the fella was supposed to interview me, yesterday? Don't say no, 'cause I seen you there." She eyed Billy suspiciously.

"Yes, I was the reporter on the story. What's wrong?" Asked Billy, as he glanced over at an exasperated Fox and a slightly bemused, though quickly tiring, Claire.

Mrs. Burke pointed to the front page, on which they had run the two top stories side by side. Both Fox and Billy had liked the setup, nice and neat, four columns each with a picture of the, as yet, unidentified Hoffman Muir and a Dominic Pierce, who was the owner and driver of the car that was struck by the young boy.

"You got the pictures mixed up or something."

Billy made a quick mental inventory of the known facts and concluded that Al must be right about her…trouble.

"What do you mean, mixed up? These are the two men the police identified in each case."

"Cain't be. That man, right there, was driving the car that went and hit that little boy. I never seen the other one." She was pointing to Hoffman Muir as the man who drove the car.

"That can't be, Mrs. Burke. That man was arrested over a mile away from your corner, not twenty minutes after the accident."

"So? Twenty minutes is twenty minutes. All I know is that I saw that man get halfway out of his car to check on the Follo child and then get back in his car and drive away like he was in some big rush."

She was still pointing to Muir and staring at Billy with a defiant glare.

"I'm sorry, but Pierce owns the car and turned up at the Police Station claiming to be the driver. He explained what happened exactly the way you did. Why would he make that up?" Asked Billy.

"Don't know. Don't care. I was there and he wasn't. Why don't you go ask him for yourself?"

Billy was getting frustrated, so he told her that he would look into it further.

"You do that. I don't think it's right that I should have to come all the way down, here, and do your job for ya. Know what I mean?"

After saying that and pausing for a moment to accentuate the imposition they had heaped upon her, she grabbed her coat off the counter and lumbered out of the building.

"Interesting woman." Claire observed as Mrs. Burke moved away from the office, towards the square.

"That's not the word I'd use." was Billy's reply.

Fox picked up the paper and examined the photos for some similarity between the two men, figuring, that if there was, she may just have misidentified Pierce. However, no matter what angle he took, the men looked nothing alike. After all, Pierce had no gray hair and only a few lines on his face, while Muir was almost entirely gray. Further, Muir, even at his advanced age, looked to be in fine physical shape, while Pierce looked like any other sixty year-old who sat on the couch, eating snacks and avoiding anything more strenuous than a walk to the kitchen for chips or cookies or beer nuts.

Still, you could not ignore the only witness to an accident. So when he got done examining the pictures, he looked at Billy, who was eyeing him, intently. "What do you think?"

"I think I'll take a little ride over to Pierce's place and ask him a few questions. I wonder if there is some part of her story that only the driver would know?" Suddenly lending some credence to what Mrs. Burke had proposed.

"I'll have to go get my car, it's back at Park Place." Billy didn't mind taking another walk, after all, he wasn't entirely focused, yet.

As Billy turned to leave, Fox interrupted him. "You said you had some insight into one of these stories. You want to brief me before you go?"

"Take too long. I'll make time when I get back."

The Homemakers Touch

Billy drove his old beat-up green Capri towards the West section of the city, where Pierce gave them an address. The streets were tight, parking on both sides. This part of the city was purely residential, two and three family homes lining both sides of the street, the pattern interrupted, only occasionally, by a small convenience store or a neighborhood school. There was a small beautification park just off Main St. and directly across from it sat 18 Baldwin Ave., one of a handful of single family dwellings in this part of the city.

Billy checked his notes to be certain he had the correct address. Satisfied, he parked his car, got out, crossed the street and walked to the front stairs. He looked around noting that the house seemed out of place, surrounded by two and three family structures on both sides. The house was small, with stone columns bordering the front stoop and a second floor porch that was slanted towards the street.

There were eight steps leading to a porch that was the width of the frontage and continued halfway along the side of the house bordered by the driveway. He looked around the corner and noticed an old decaying garage, a reddish rust color, different from the brown of the house, itself. A window sat above the garage opening, a loft for storage above the carport.

There were wooden shingles, in good repair covering the exterior of the house. The side along the driveway had three windows on the first floor and three on the second, two embedded in the foundation illuminating a finished cellar.

The porch itself had two windows, one on either side of a large wooden door. Through one of the windows Billy could see an almost empty Living room. Two chairs, one a folding chair, sat in the middle of the room with a snack table and a large console television, rabbit ears adorning the top, being the only other items of furniture. Into the hallway beyond, he saw a desk upon which sat a small computer that was, at the moment turned off.

He pushed the doorbell, heard it's cry echo about inside and waited. There was no reply. He looked into the mailbox and found two or three pieces, all addressed to Pierce, two looking like utility bills while a third looked like a business envelope from SG Enterprises. He was tempted to take the envelope, but didn't.

After he had pushed the doorbell two or three times, with no reply, he decided to try the back of the house. He went down the front stairs and was going to go around to the driveway, when he noticed that the rubbish containers were on the other side. He went in that direction. Once at the barrels, he gave a quick look inside, finding one envelope from the same SG Enterprises. Unfortunately there was nothing that looked like it could have been inside it.

Once done ferreting through the trash he walked around to the back, climbing the steps and peering through a window set in the back door. He could see the back hallway, which was empty. There was no bell, so he knocked on the door, again, getting no response. The hallway led to a kitchen that was lit by a beam of light coming from a window above the sink. He could see a small table and three chairs.

From his angle he couldn't see counters or any of the usual appliances. He studied the room for anything of interest, but mostly, as with the front of the house, the room seemed devoid of any true signs of life. He thought about the sparseness of the furnishings and concluded that there was nothing that said someone lived, here, someone felt at home, here, someone had ties to this property.

He backed away from the door, still staring through the window for a glimmer of life. He brushed the back railing and as he did he stepped on a crumpled piece of paper. He opened it. It was a part of a Bank Statement. There was no name or account number visible, but the name of the bank, The Everett Trust Company, was printed on the corner of the document. He folded the paper and put it in his pocket.

In the driveway he stared at the large garage. From the looks of it, it was not used very often. There was a rusted pad lock on the front door, but none on the side entrance. Probably a storage facility of some sort, either for the owners or the current tenants, he thought to himself.

He stepped back, away from the door and noticed that there were no windows on the ground floor. In fact, aside from one window above the front door, there were no windows, at all. Peering down the driveway he didn't see anyone so he decided to try the side door. He tried to turn the knob but it was locked. He didn't think there was any reason to try and force it.

He walked around to the back of the garage, noticing an old push lawn mower and some old style wood molding; wet and rotting, nails protruded and rusted. The chain link fence that surrounded the property was decrepit, bent in several places and, here, broken through. The overall condition of the property, inside and out, was neglected.

Billy had seen enough. He decided to leave and turned towards the driveway when he came face to face with Al who gave him a questioned look.

"Inspecting the property or are you trying to became a PI on your own?"

"Pete's enough. What's up?"

The two men walked back towards the street along the driveway side of the house. Al told Billy that he had called the office and Fox explained the problem related to the pictures that ran with this morning's stories.

"So? What do you think of her story, Al?"

They stopped at the end of the driveway, Al staring at the upper floors of the house.

"I just don't know. The woman's trouble, has been for a long time. Nothing she ever complains about is verified. She once called 911 because two men were trying to break into her place after they had just sacked the house next door. Turns out, the two guys were a fifteen year old kid and his dad, doing missionary work for the Mormons."

"I knew you were going to say something like that, but she sounded pretty certain, so I thought I'd check it out."

Al shook his head, then with his hands in his pockets turned and surveyed the street, before looking back at Billy.

"What's the place look like? Anything to worry about?"

“I don’t know, but everything about this place looks funny to me.”

“How so?”

“There’s practically no furniture in the front room or the kitchen, everything seems to be rotting away and the trash cans don’t look like they’ve been emptied in weeks.”

“Lousy landlord.”

Billy was not amused. He watched as Al climbed the front steps and peered through one of the windows. When he returned he shrugged his shoulders.

“Why would a guy lie about hitting a little boy?”

Billy had no answer, but, now, he was certain that Mrs. Burke was telling the truth. Everything about what he had seen, here, made no sense. If he hadn’t known any better, he would have thought that the house was vacant.

“I don’t know, Al. I just don’t know.”

“Well, I’ll keep tabs on this place and if this guy, Pierce, resurfaces, I’ll have a talk with him.”

They both walked to their cars, Billy across the street, Al right in front of the house. Al was pulling away from the curb as Billy settled in behind the wheel. Al stopped his car and motioned Billy to roll down his window.

"Listen, don't you talk to this guy on your own. Let me do it. I'll keep you up to date. If this guy wasn't the driver, then the guy who broke into Blake's room was and that means a whole different kind of trouble. We on the same page, here?"

"No promises, Sarge. Now get outta here!"

As Al drove away, Billy smiled to himself, bemused by Al's protective instincts. However, that mood changed when Billy began to think of what Blake had told him the night before. Billy was beginning to see the larger picture. Pierce turned himself in for a crime he didn't commit. The unknown man, he reasoned, would have had to commit both the break-in and the hit and run. And, if he was after Blake or his notes or something Blake had, it wouldn't be too far fetched to assume that he had something to do with two murders.

The Everett Trust

Alex was seated at a computer terminal in the High School computer lab, assisting a student with a graphic arts program when Billy let himself in. School was still in session, the noon break approaching, so he sat at her desk and waited for the bell.

Alex looked up and saw him, smiling she gave him a little wave as she moved from one student to the next. She had been teaching computer sciences for the last couple of years, running the lab and training both students and teachers on the virtues of personal computing. Prior to her tenure in the lab she had taught English to college-bound eleventh and twelfth graders.

She was fascinated by the free and fast flow of information now possible through an ever-widening array of electronic wonders. While Billy and Pete harbored an irrational fear of these powerful machines, she embraced them and made them a necessary part of her everyday life, constantly espousing the benefits of high technology to her less enthusiastic friends. Taking control of the computer lab was a logical extension for her as no one else seemed to be so inclined.

The bell rang precisely at noon, students rising and disappearing within seconds of the first tone. With the exception of the unlucky student with whom she was working at the time, the lab was empty before the bell had completed its cycle. Finally, she was done with the last student and she turned her attention to Billy.

"So what's up? You taking me to lunch?"

Billy got out of her seat as she approached the desk.

"No. But that's not a bad idea."

"Okay, then...what's the favor?"

Billy laughed, as she sat down, putting papers into neat little stacks and rearranging them into some meaningful order.

"I need you to look someone up at the bank, tonight."

Alex shook her head and smiled as if pleased with the fact that she could read her friend so well. She opened a drawer and pulled out her purse, stood up and started to head for the door.

"How about that lunch?" She asked.

Billy bowed graciously, and pointed towards the door. Alex a step ahead of him, left the room and he followed.

They exited the building on a side street and quickly walked to Broadway, where they crossed amid still moving traffic and entered a small diner across from the front of the school. The place was crowded with students throwing money at the counter and demanding sub sandwiches of all sizes and concoctions. Alex caught the eye of one of the men behind the counter and nodded before she and Billy sat at a table situated near the entrance to the rest rooms.

As they took off their coats, the same young man appeared with two cups of coffee and one menu. He placed the coffees in front of them and gave the menu to Billy. He looked at Alex and simply said the word: "salad".

"Caesar. It's on him."

Billy looked up and nodded. The waiter wrote the order down and waited for Billy to tell him that he wanted a Cheese Steak sub before disappearing into the crowd in front of the counter. All around, Billy could see and hear the sights and sounds of teens at play; loud talk, loud music, loud dress and loud and exaggerated gestures.

"So, who's the bad guy?" Alex teased. Alex worked most afternoons as an Assistant Manager at the Everett Trust. Billy told her what he had found at Pierce's and asked her to look into his finances.

"What am I looking for?"

"I'm not sure, but if this Burke woman is correct, he's got something to hide."

Their lunches were brought to the table and they began to eat. Alex kept staring out the window beyond Billy.

"What's on your mind?" He asked.

"Is there something you haven't told me?"

"Not really. I haven't put all the pieces together yet, but I don't think there's anything to worry about."

"That's what I thought you'd say. What's really up?"

"We may have stumbled onto something a bit more complex than just a simple break-in. I had a long talk with Blake last night and he convinced me that there's something going on here that's pretty strange."

"Such as?"

"Let me worry about that for now."

"Well, I shouldn't agree to help you unless you tell me, but as long as you tell me you'll be careful..."

"I don't know that there is anything to worry about just yet. So relax. Just look into this guy and call me at Pete's later on."

"Alright."

They completed their lunches, drank their coffee and left the diner; Alex walking back into the High School and Billy heading back to the paper. As he walked away, he watched Alex cross the street. She was tall, taught and strong, an athletic build. One or two of her students stopped her to chat and she was all smiles as she eagerly answered their questions. Soon she was surrounded by students, disappearing into a maze of teenagers heading back into the building.

Upon returning to his office, Billy decided to tell Fox everything. He thought that Fox could put everything into its proper perspective. At the very least, he would get to sound it out before he explained it to Pete.

Once inside, he saw Fox was on the phone. An old Washington friend, Samuel Prine, had called out of the blue to see how Fox was doing. Fox hadn't spoken to Prine in over a year so the timing of the call was suspicious, at best. Billy asked Claire what was up and when she told him that it was an old Washington friend, he, too, figured it was more than a coincidence.

The Call

Fox had built a great many contacts throughout the DC area including many within the government apparatus. Prine was a man of some weight at the Justice Department. He had heard of the previous day's events and as this was the first time Fox had had a story go semi-national, it was the first time he had thought of his friend in quite a while.

Fox wasn't buying it. He had been around long enough to know when he was being snowed, even by a pro. Prine was more interested with the break-in. He had heard that Blake was the intended target and said something about not being so sure that thwarting the robbery was such a good idea. They both laughed; Prine louder and longer.

Billy watched as Fox terminated the call, hanging up the phone and looking over at Claire with a familiar laugh. He saw Billy sitting at the edge of his seat.

"These guys never change. This one, Samuel W. Prine, is a Director of some section of the Justice Department, I can't remember which...anyway, he called to see how I was doing and whether or not anyone had called in the Feds on this break-in. I told him he should be asking Roselli that question."

"Oh great! That's sure gonna put me on solid footing with him."

"Don't worry. He has no intention of calling Roselli. He wanted to know what I knew. Trying to get a feel for how things work around here."

"Why would he care about that?" Billy had an idea, but he hadn't had the chance to tell Fox about Blake's story.

"Ordinarily he wouldn't, but, for some reason, he's interested in the break-in…or should I say, the perp."

Claire got up and walked over to the coffee machine and poured one for her and another for Fox. "I doubt that anything, here, would be of interest to the Justice Department."

"If I hadn't spent forty years in Washington I would agree with you. But, if there's anything I've learned from my experiences there, it's that they have an interest in everything."

"You think, he knows the perp?" Billy was thinking out loud. He was reasoning that if the break-in is related to two murders in Louisiana and Florida, then there was a good chance that someone in Washington could easily make the same connection.

He decided that this was the best time to let Fox know what he and Blake had discussed the night before. "I told you Blake stopped by last night."

"What he want?" Asked an extremely curious Fox.

"He wanted to talk. We went out for a bite and he gave me the nuts and bolts of his story. I know he held something back, but what he gave me was pretty compelling."

"I'm sure you're not supposed to be telling me what you're about to tell me...right?"

"Something like that. But I've got to bounce it off someone, so here goes..."

With that, Billy told Fox about the smuggling operation, the theft of weaponry from the armory, the contacts to both Organized crime and the State Department, the two murders and the fact that the victim in Florida once worked for the CIA.

When he was done, Fox told Billy that Prine had asked about whether or not Blake was doing a story about the Organization of American States. Fox no longer thought it was a curious question.

"I think Blake said the guy who died in Chicago was involved with the OAS."

"I'm not sure what we've got, but we've got something that smells bad."

Claire had been standing off to the side, listening, when she remembered Fox's coffee. She placed it in front of him and then went back to one of the computers, near enough so she could continue to listen while she tapped away on the keyboard.

"Do we know who this guy in South Florida was?"

"Hayes was his name."

"You say he was in his seventies?"

"Yea. Why? Do you know who this guy is?"

"Maybe. I knew of a CIA plant down there, running a program called JMWave right before the Missile Crisis. I may have met him, too."

"Did you cover that story?"

"Everyone covered that story."

As Billy and Fox exchanged questions, Claire was busy reading a story in the Times Picayune, the New Orleans daily, about the death of Cabrerra.

"You think this is the same Hayes?" Billy asked.

"Got to be. How many people by that name, taught at Miami, worked for the CIA and would be that old?"

"You're probably right." As Billy said that, Claire interrupted them.

"Boys! I've got something you might want to read."

Billy and Fox walked over to her terminal and began to read. The story detailed very little about the murder, though a quote from one of the investigating officers relating to the professional nature of the "hit" drew everyone's attention. Beyond that, the article spent several paragraphs detailing Cabrerra's anti-Castro politics in both Miami and New Orleans. In fact, Fernando Cabrerra had once been arrested after a heated argument with Lee Harvey Oswald on a New Orleans street corner. The argument was a confrontation between ideological viewpoints; Cabrerra arguing that Castro should be thrown out of Cuba, Oswald arguing that Castro was a visionary and should be left alone in his attempts to build a better Cuba.

Cabrerra had also been arrested in the Louisiana Bayou, along with several other Cuban ex-patriots, by the FBI and Federal marshals during raids made on suspected CIA-backed gorilla training sites. By the late sixties, Cabrerra had become a fixture in Miami's Little Havana, a proprietor of a small cafe where older Cubans came to swap tales of forays onto Cuban soil and map out plans to keep pressure on Castro.

"One fascinating old man." The voice was Pete's. He had crept up behind Billy and Fox. "Why the interest?"

Billy, uncertain as to how much he should tell Pete, looked to Fox.

"We just stumbled upon it." Claire pushed the "print" button and cleared the screen.

"What's up?" Billy felt a little pang of guilt, but figured he'd be bringing Pete into his confidence soon enough.

"I just ran into Al and he says old lady Burke thinks you need help doing your job. I figure it's a soft gig, so, here I am."

"Very funny."

"No, I'm serious. Where do you want me to look?"

Billy stared at Pete, deciding only to tell him that he had reason to believe that the situation was more serious than just a simple case of mistaken identity. While he really didn't want to compromise his word to Blake, he had his own story to write. Both stories were obviously connected. What if the murderer was in town?

"I'll be honest with you. I don't know where to start. But finding out what the connection between Pierce and our mystery guest would seem like a good place." Billy declared.

"I'm on it." Pete asked a couple of questions about the two men and when Billy told him that he had asked Alex to look into the bank account, Pete was anxious to get started, himself. "I bet if I tail Blake, he'll lead me to one or the other. Otherwise, it's sit quiet and wait outside Pierce's digs."

Fox rose from his chair. "If you tail him, remember he's a pro."

"You, sir, have insulted the master. I'm nothing if not invisible."

"Just be careful, okay?"

"You're telling me something, Scoop? What's with Blake?"

"I'll get into that later. For now just watch yourself."

Pete studied Billy and didn't like the fact that he felt like he was being cut out of something. No matter, he thought, Billy would never put him in harm's way.

Chapter Five

Fox In The Hen House

Pete made a couple of phone calls before leaving. He thought he had a good line on Blake, so he left telling Billy that he would meet him later that evening. Billy turned his attention to Fox, asking him if he had any ideas on where the story was really heading.

"Down that dark alley you were told to avoid. This has all the markings of one of those dangerous stories that keep unfolding more sinister layers the deeper you dig."

"We've both been down that road."

Claire asked Billy if he were up to it. He paused and reflected. It had been a long time since Buffalo, but the idea of real reporting was starting to intrigue him, again.

"I'm way beyond being up to it, Claire."

She smiled, walked over to him and gave him motherly hug around the shoulders, catching him by surprise. She kissed the top of his head, then walked back to the coffee machine, brushing Fox's shoulder as she passed.

"This conversation reminds me of my first big story. I was supposed to be covering the 1960 Republican convention. I was sure it was an unevent so I tried to posture myself out of the assignment. My editor spent two weeks laughing at me as I came up with one lousy story idea after another trying to get out of it.

Finally, I got a break. Some guy from the Pentagon committed suicide three days before I was supposed to go. The suicide was my story, so I put it together and out it went. I read the story in the paper, that night, and it didn't feel right, so I made a call to an old college mate of mine who worked on Capital Hill. He told me the guy was being targeted by a Congressional Committee.

Seems they thought he had been pushing some questionable contracts, one of which led to a test pilot's death. Nothing struck me right away. But while doing some background work, I had the chance to interview the bereaved widow. Only, she wasn't so bereaved. He had had a lovely little playmate hidden away in Virginia.

I followed the trail and it led me to a fashionable address in Falls Church. Once there, I found another Coroner. No one made any connection between her falling from the balcony of her Penthouse and the suicide, but me. I knew. I laid it out for my editor and he let me out of the convention and told me to stick with the story."

Fox paused and stared past Billy, moving right on to the schoolyard across the street. He was struck by a man leaning against the building, wearing a raincoat, broad rimmed hat and dark glasses. In New York or DC, even Boston, he would not have made any impression, but here he was in Everett and that made him stick out.

"The story. Finish the story."

Claire saw where Fox was looking and, she, too, thought he was a little odd. From across the schoolyard she could see flecks of gray, but nothing more. Billy turned to see what was up, but as he turned, the man stepped behind the building and disappeared down a side street.

"What's that all about?" Billy said as he saw him disappear behind the school. "I'm on it! Call Al!"

"Where do you think you're going?!" Cried Claire, as Billy ran to the door. "Don't get too close!"

Fox stood and simply stared out of the window. He watched Billy cross the street, run across the schoolyard and disappear around the corner. Claire had, by now, called Al and was attempting to see where Billy had gone.

"Aren't you going to follow him?"

"What do you expect me to do? He's no fool, he won't confront him. Trust me."

"Charles! Make certain he's alright!"

Fox shook his head and slowly made his way to the door, when Billy reappeared. He was out of breath and a bit disheveled. Billy looked at the ground around the spot where the mysterious man had been standing. Fox made his way over to him and asked what he had seen.

Billy told him that he only saw the man's coat tails as he headed down an alley and into the parking lot behind the main city parking lot. There, the man got into a car that was already running and pulled away. He didn't get close enough to see the make or model and certainly didn't see a license plate. The color was white and it looked like a newer model, but that was about all.

Then Billy looked at Fox and said, "He was here a little while." They looked down at the ground where three cigarette butts lay. Fox looked back at Claire, who was standing on the top step as a squad car pulled up. Al jumped out and ran to where Billy and Fox were standing.

"What's going on?"

Fox looked up from the ground. "Someone has been watching the paper."

"Did you get a good look at him?"

"Not really, he was covered up pretty good."

"What about you, Bill?"

"I really only saw him flee around the corner. I chased him, but I never got close enough to see anything useful."

Fox had walked away and was crossing the street. Al picked up the cigarette butts and then he and Billy walked across the street. Once inside, they all sat down, Al nervously tapping on the desktop in front of him.

"How do I write it up?"

"It doesn't matter, Al. The real question is why would they watch us?"

Fox walked back to the coffee machine. "Billy, I think they were watching you. Somebody's nervous."

"It doesn't matter who they were watching. I'm going to get you some protection." Al grabbed the phone while he was saying that and dialed the station.

"If we don't find out who that guy is pretty soon, it won't help." Fox poured his coffee and stared towards the back of the room.

Dining in Public

Pete traveled north on Broadway, past the old cemetery, the elderly housing complex, an old scrap metal yard; towards the Hospitality Hotel. He had called an old friend still employed there, inquiring whether or not Blake was in the building. He was told that he was having lunch with two men.

Pete pulled his car into the lot and parked away from the front entrance, as he always did when visiting a client or friend staying there. Because he had been asked to leave the employ of the hotel under less than friendly terms, he was not a welcome visitor. For his part, he stayed away, not frequenting the lounge or the restaurant, musing that the decision to can him had cost some poor bartender a lot of easy money.

He parked out by the trash bins, in back, near where the laundry trucks came and went, not wanting to announce his presence. He walked straight to the restaurant, where he met his friend and asked to be seated quietly; across the room from Blake's table. Once seated, he ordered a scotch and then, fastened his attention on Blake and his two companions.

Much to his surprise, he recognized both men. A tall athletic red-haired man, in his early thirties was known as Scooter Morse from his days as a shifty running back at Boston College before a ruptured Achilles tendon turned him into one of Boston's top Private Investigators. There were rumors that he had used money squeezed into his palms on cold rainy fall afternoons in the Eagles locker room at the Heights, to set up shop. One or two agents might have come around at the start of his senior year, before his injury and made promises that were never to be kept, advancing money that would never be repaid.

Now, Morse, with the help of two friends, had become one of the most successful investigators in the city. He made his name protecting the city's most famous personalities; from pro athletes to politicos to the unknown wealthy to the high society chic. Three years ago he had single-handedly thwarted an abduction attempt of a wealthy prep school student. That put him on the map and made his agency the one to contract for any matter that fell within his ever-expanding areas of expertise.

The other gentleman was known to Pete, as well. His name was Doherty and he was a Union man. Officially a Union officer, he was the man who controlled the docks in Chelsea and

Charlestown with power behind him that was unchallenged. He had been investigated by every new Suffolk County DA since the early sixties. A keen political sense always had his hand in the right pockets. He frequented the right bars and pubs, establishing a power base from the lads who labored on the docks and made their living fishing, hauling and trafficking. If you wanted to know what was really going on at the docks all you had to do was ask Ed Doherty.

Pete was beginning to grant Blake a certain amount of credit for knowing who the players were and for getting their attention. Pete had had run-ins with both of these guys before and he knew how tough it was to deal with them.

For his part, Pete stared at the trio through the bottom of his ever empty glass wishing he had some way of listening to their conversation. What he could see was of little use to him. Morse handed Blake some papers, which Blake examined, then folded and tucked into an inside jacket pocket. Doherty didn't move a muscle. He sat and stared at Blake the entire time without uttering a word or making a motion.

However, Pete was certain that the simple fact of these three men having lunch together would mean something to Billy, who he knew was holding something back. Quite often, Billy seemed to forget that Pete served with military intelligence during the Vietnam War, until he was asked to leave that job, as well.

Pete watched them for almost twenty minutes before they finished their business and left the restaurant. He would follow Blake for the rest of the day. It started slow as Blake went up to his room and Pete had a short run-in with the current security officer. Knowing that Blake had a rental, he waited for him outside.

Once Blake started to move Pete was right behind him. He followed him through the outskirts of town, heading towards the coast, into Chelsea. Blake headed for the waterfront, ducking down a back alley and parking by an old abandoned warehouse situated, almost, directly under the Tobin Bridge.

Chelsea was a city divided by the bridge and the highway that extended across the river into the Charlestown section of Boston. It severed the city into two large sections, dividing neighborhoods and isolating the waterfront area from the rest of the city.

The waterfront was once a vibrant part of the city, but as the port of Boston fell into disrepair and the volume of large cargo ships declined, Chelsea became less and less of a center of commerce and more of an impoverished urban area. The long-time residents looked at the bridge as a symbol of the gradual destruction of the city they once loved.

Eventually, the inner harbor channel was deepened and the port facilities in Charlestown and South Boston were upgraded to handle the larger ships. The port regained some of its lost luster. Chelsea, however, was never a part of the harbor renewal. It's docks and warehouses were deteriorating, leaving a few small businesses and a lot of vacant lots.

The area where Blake parked housed several old decrepit buildings and was bordered by the largest of the open parcels where once stood a hotel where sailors stayed after long voyages and danced with the local girls in the large ballroom to the sounds of live orchestras. Now there was rubble, the hotel long since destroyed and all remnants of the glorious nightlife relegated to the few remaining memories of the older generation, now, trying to move away from the old neighborhoods.

Pete pulled over a block or so behind Blake and quickly got out and followed him down an alleyway that led to the street that bordered the docks. Blake walked another block to a spot across the street from a two-story metal and tar paper shack that looked as though one more winter storm would send it into the harbor. The sign outside the fenced-in parking area read: Bonner Fishing Company.

There was one door with a window on either side and a sloped porch attached to the second floor that wrapped around the building to the rear. Behind the building was a decaying wooden wharf with an old fishing vessel tied to the supports and listing, slightly, in the harbor. There were two cars in the lot, but there were no visible signs of life.

Blake sat on the retaining wall of an old apartment building and watched. Pete ducked into a stairwell of the building next to it. He looked across the harbor and noticed that from their vantage point the city of Boston looked absolutely beautiful. Boston was a red city, brick buildings showing off its subtler charms at almost any angle from which the city was viewed. From Chelsea the newer waterfront hotels and restored warehouses, now serving as up-scale condominiums and office space, deflected a warm glow in the late afternoon sun.

There they sat, watching the old fish company, waiting for something to happen. Pete glanced at his watch, from time to time, as the day passed into dusk and eventually into early evening. Blake did not stir from his perch until the sun had faded and the cool evening air off the water had changed the mild Spring afternoon into a bone chilling night. Around eight, Blake got up to leave. Pete hid while he walked past, deciding that he had had enough and would take up the chase, again, in the morning.

A Dog's Life

Captain Roselli was a man of few distractions, his favorite being a quiet evening with some acquaintances at the local Dog Track. He was regularly off duty by seven and since the first race went off promptly at 7:05 he had time to go home, eat a sparse supper and get to the track before the meat of the evening had begun. He hated missing the daily double, but one of his friends would play his numbers on the nights he was sure to be there. That would be two or three times a week.

Roselli was not from Everett, he had no family in the area and few friends. After twenty years, there, he still preferred the company of other officers. He had been a widower for almost fifteen years. He had tried a couple of relationships in the intervening years but neither of the women could get used to the idea that he was a police officer. Now, set in his ways and tired from years of pressure and tension he had resigned himself to a solitary life save for a son, living on the west coast whom he rarely saw.

He structured his time and limited his vulnerability. He took up going to the track several years ago. Over the last couple of years he had made friends of three retired men, all either government or military men, like himself.

Tonight, he had more than just diversion on his mind when he met the guys. Harry Blair was an old colleague of Roselli, his commanding officer during his tour of duty in Vietnam. He had run into him at the track one night and after catching up on old times he started looking for him every time he went. Blair had retired, moved into a condo on Revere Beach and started coming to the track almost every night when it was in session.

Through Blair he met Gil Holland and Arthur Cogent, both retired government men, both in their seventies and both cranky, arrogant and connected. Many nights they would sit in the clubhouse, lay down small bets and talk of all the important matters of the day. For four guys sitting in a racetrack, they never discussed their bets or handicapped races for each other, or talked any sports at all. It was always politics and international intrigue.

This is what drew Roselli to this aging band of miscreants. He knew that both Holland and Cogent were connected at the highest levels of government. Harry had told him that both men were well known in Washington and always seemed to have amazing insights to the back room dealings and negotiated compromises of government.

Tonight, he had an agenda. He wanted to know who they had released and he thought that one of these old men would have the means to find out. Upon arriving, there were the initial pleasantries and queries into the current states of each individual's life. As usual, this passed quickly and uneventfully.

Roselli laid down a small wager on the three dog in the fourth race without even opening his program. Cogent, chomping on his favorite cigar, watched Roselli out of the corner of his eye. He could see he was not himself, a little agitated, a little distracted. As they watched the race on the monitor at their table, they never ventured outside to actually watch a race, Cogent kept one eye on his dog and the other on the good Captain.

The race ended, the three dog hopelessly out of the picture before they turned for home, both Holland and Blair cashing Place bets on the six dog. They excused themselves and went to collect their winnings and place them on the next race. Cogent had a winner, as well, but opted to stay at the table.

"What's on your mind Cap? Sour taste in your mouth?"

"Maybe a little, Arthur, maybe a little."

"A little? Who the hell are you kidding? You put a ten spot on a pig you used to say should be glazed and baked for a Sunday dinner."

Roselli laughed a bit, remembering that he had, indeed, bet on a dog that he had always hated.

Cogent continued, looking over the top edge of his glasses perched at the tip of his nose; "I heard about your uninvited guest. Things getting a little warm in Everett, are they?"

"You know anything about that, Arthur?"

"I might. A few words have passed my way in the last couple of days."

"Do you know who this guy is?"

Blair and Holland returned to the table and could see the seriousness on Roselli's face.

Blair leaned in on Cogent. "What have you said this time?"

"I was just commenting on the notoriety his department has gotten the last couple of days, that's all?"

"Do you know him? It's important!" Roselli stood and glared at his friend.

"Sit down Cap. If I knew his name I would already have told you."

Gil Holland had been sitting quietly during their exchange, until; "Who do you think it is?"

"If I had any idea, I wouldn't be asking for help." He sat down, again.

Holland looked at Cogent for a moment and then shook his head. "Damned if I know who this guy is. But I'll tell you one thing, he's not local. My friends in DC tell me that something's going down and that you don't want to get caught in the middle of it."

"Such as?"

"Don't know. My guess is it's a Federal thing. You know this state is lousy with Feds. And that reporter, Blake, is easily one of the most hated men in America. So there's any number of people who might want to know what he's working on. My guess is you find out what he's doing, here, and you'll know."

"That much I surmised. But Blake isn't going to tell us anything."

"Maybe, not voluntarily." Cogent had taken his glasses off and was rubbing his eyes as he spoke.

"I won't even be drawn into that discussion."

Harry was getting nervous. Through the years, he had seen Roselli agitated many times. This time he was taking it personal; never a good sign with the Captain. Cogent, on the other hand, was enjoying the moment a bit too much, for his liking, and that, too, needed to be defused.

He found himself suggesting that they might call it an early night. Cogent and Holland, reluctantly, agreed, but Cogent was definitely disappointed. He had often gotten into heated arguments with Roselli, both being opinionated men. This time he could sense that it was different.

He was right. Maybe Everett was a small town to men like Cogent, but it was Roselli's town and he didn't like the feeling of being played for an unimportant, ignorant fool.

As Roselli walked to the exit, Harry walked with him.

"Don't get upset with old Arthur, he's not used to following any rules."

"Just what is he used to?"

"Someday, maybe I'll tell you. But for now, just know that he's not a man to be trifled with. He's got friends in the shadows."

"God, Harry, who is this guy?"

"Retired CIA. That's all I can tell you."

Roselli looked back at the table. Cogent and Holland were having a belly laugh about something. As he walked away, he lost the sound of their laughter in the din of the activity around him.

A Late Night Snack

It was close to nine when Pete got back to his apartment. Billy and Alex were already there, eating take out and comparing notes. Pete was tired and hungry, not having eaten since lunch. He grabbed a handful of wings and a beer before sitting down at his favorite spot on his couch.

"So, where are we?" Pete would attempt to catch up.

"I was just telling Billy that Pierce has a very unusual checking account."

"How so?" asked Pete?

"He gets two ACH deposits, each month, for $3,000.00 each"

"Are you serious? What kind of gig does he have?"

"The funds are deposited from an offshore account. I have a friend who claims to be able to find out where the funds come from. But I won't hold my breath."

Billy put down his coffee and focused his attention on Pete.

"What did you find out?"

"I followed Blake the whole day. First, he had lunch with Scooter Morse and Ed Doherty of the Longshoreman's Union."

"Wonder where they fit in with all of this." Mused Alex.

"I've got some ideas."

Pete knew that Billy had some idea of what was going on, but for now he was content to wait. He had decided that he wouldn't press Billy...for now.

"After that, he went down to the Chelsea waterfront and sat across the street from the Bonner Fish Company for the rest of the afternoon. No one came or went. So we just sat there until a little while ago.

"Now, Billy, what does all this mean?" Pete figured, now was a good time to find out what everyone knew. He didn't think Billy would keep him in the dark for too long if he truly knew something that the others didn't.

"Well, first, it would be great if we could find out where that money is coming from. Anything else we can learn from that account?"

Alex looked through her notes and then looked at Billy. "You cut me off before I could tell you the most interesting thing. There is no activity except for ATM withdrawals...aside from one check made out to Serino's Storage on the Parkway."

"Storage? I wonder what he would need storage space for? I went over to his house and there was almost nothing in it. Plus, there was a whole garage, there, that was empty."

The three of them looked at each other for a moment.

"You went to school with one of the Serino girls, didn't you?" Asked Billy.

"Yea, well, that was a long time ago and I haven't exactly been keeping in touch with her since then."

"I'm asking just in case we need to take a look at that storage bin."

Billy got up and refilled both his and Alex's mugs. Then he sat down and told them about his conversation with Blake. He told them about the stolen weapons, the offshore transfer of, what he believed to be guns for drugs, the two murders and that he believed Organized crime was in the middle of it.

Then he told them about the man who was watching the paper, and finally;

"Al's going to provide some kind of protection for me."

"I can and should do that. There's no reason to get Al involved."

"I want you to stick with Blake. He's the only person that knows the full scope of what's really going on, here...No, I want you to stay on him. Let Al worry about protection."

"Listen to the two of you." Shouted Alex. "I want us to get out of this, now! If you think we might be dealing with a killer, then I want you to drop this."

"Alex, how can I not continue to cover this story? Its the biggest thing we've had, here, in years."

Pete offered, "Not since the mob car bombed that lawyer back in the sixties, anyway."

"That's comforting. Why don't you try to calm her nerves." Billy was not amused. He believed he needed Alex's help and didn't want to alienate her.

"Don't worry, Alex. Al's on it. Besides, we're not sure that everything is connected, yet. I would guess that if someone is in danger, it's probably Blake."

The three friends finished their meals without talking for a few minutes. Pete was on his third beer when the phone rang. It was Al and he wanted to let Billy know that Roselli hadn't approved the protection. He told Billy that Roselli said that there was no evidence that he was in any danger. He told Billy that he would keep pressure on Roselli to change his mind and that he would be looking out for him, in the meantime. In fact, he told him he would meet him at his office in the morning to get an idea of what Billy had planned for the day.

Billy didn't want to tell either of them, especially Alex. Instead, he simply told them that Al was going to meet him in the morning.

"What do you want me to do tomorrow, anything?" Alex wanted to help, but knew that there would be little that she could do.

"I'm not sure. Stay on your friend and see if he really can find out where that money is coming from."

Billy's biggest concern was for Pete to continue on Blake's trail while he and Fox worked the Washington angle. Billy was thinking that too many little bits and pieces of information related to Washington's hidden power. He was worried that Blake was scratching surfaces that wouldn't appreciate his prying eyes.

For now, he would keep those concerns to himself.

*****

It was after midnight when Billy drove Alex home and retired to his own apartment knowing sleep would not come easily for him. Rather than go to bed he grabbed a comforter and sat, outside, on his balcony. His mind was racing. He had formed an uneasy alliance with Blake and wondered whether he was in over his head. He wondered about his own abilities, his own senses, his own desire to handle the big story. He wasn't even sure what to do with the big story.

A part of him wasn't even certain that he wanted to handle a big story, after all this time. Memories began to surface, to haunt him. All the years of allowing his talents to go unused, to forego his career and ambitions for the security of home and friends left a great deal of doubt within him. Did he have the edge he used to have? He knew he didn't. Was his desire to push himself, this one last time, a mistake? Would there be another chance or should he just come to grips with the fact that he no longer had what it took to succeed as a writer?

Over the years he had gotten more and more used to being just a local newsman. He had begun to believe he had settled where he, actually, belonged. That, here, he would not have to push himself, just to fail, in the end. It had been too long since he allowed, himself, the luxury of feeling important.

He had forgotten that he was once one of the most sought after young reporters on the east coast. And that after he had returned from Buffalo he got offers, for a time, from some of the largest newspapers around. But he had rolled himself up into a ball of guilt, insecurity and self-pity. So, still not over Terry's death and still feeling sorry for himself, he never acted on any of them.

After a couple of years the offers stopped coming. He was all but forgotten by the news establishment, all but forgotten by anyone outside his own hometown. For a long while he thought he had found peace, comfort and release from the overwhelming guilt. But that too, was gone once Fox bought the paper and excited those long-forgotten energies, that spark of desire, that old burning to make a difference with his words.

As he stared at his favorite view of his beloved city, all he could think about was the conflict raging inside: Did he want to be a reporter, again or was he content to let this last chance slide through his fingers without the fear that he couldn't handle it anymore?

The night air was colder than the last few nights but snuggled up in a warm comforter and staring at a world that meant so much to him, he felt no chill. Consumed with his thoughts, confronted by old ghosts, excited by new opportunities and fighting a self-doubt fueled by layers of rust and years of neglect, he, eventually, fell off into a restless sleep. The same restless sleep he had been having for the last twenty years.

Chapter Six

Doubts

When Billy awoke, he found himself in his own bed, not remembering when the cold night air forced him to return inside. He glanced at the clock, realized he was late and scampered into the shower. He let the warm water pound his neck and shoulders, the feeling, almost prolonging the comfort of his bed.

By the time he was dressed and ready to face the day, it was too late for any breakfast so he grabbed a jacket and headed for one of the three doughnut shops he would pass on his way to the office. Having secured a cup of coffee and two plain doughnuts he made his way to the paper.

When he reached the office he was disappointed to find that Fox was already there. He had hoped that he wouldn't have to explain why he was late, since he didn't have a reason that he could put out into words.

Fox greeted him with a robust "Hello", which Billy barely acknowledged. He sat down at his desk, brought his PC on-line and tried to wolf down one of his doughnuts.

"Something wrong, Bill?" Fox was watching him closely.

"No, not really. Just had some trouble sleeping last night."

"Pretty common, these days." Fox had noticed, on several mornings that Billy had looked less than rested. The frequency seemed to be increasing over the last several months. Billy just grunted.

Fox decided to try a different tack; "What did Alex find out about that bank account?"

"It's a little strange."

"Strange, how?" Billy told Fox about the deposits, the single check and the meeting he, Alex and Pete had had the night before. He also told Fox that he was concerned about safety. Fox was visibly upset when told that Al had not been able to provide the promised protection. They were on their own.

"That puts a different spin on it. Maybe I'll give that Roselli a call, myself."

"You can if you want to, but I've got a feeling he's got his own vision of the world and he's at the center of it." Billy, trying not to look up at Fox, started to type.

"Any new insights to report?" Fox asked.

"Not really. I'm working on my column." Billy was just trying to stay away from the story.

"You don't have anything new to report?"

"Something like that." Billy was almost whispering.

"You know a lot more than we reported in yesterday's edition…a lot more!"

"That may be, but we're no closer to the guy's identity."

"Maybe not, but I would expect you to tell the public what you have and let them decide what to make of it." Fox was very surprised because Billy's unbridled enthusiasm of yesterday had disappeared, replaced by caution and fear. He had seen Billy like this many times and nothing good had ever come out of one of these moods.

In the past he had tried to snap him out of it by challenging him to a feature. Now, he knew that strategy wouldn't work because Billy had a pretty good story sitting in his lap.

"Why don't you stop what you're doing and tell me what's on your mind."

Billy paused and then turned to Fox. “I’m not sure where to take this. I mean, some old woman walks in here and tells us we’ve got things backwards and we start flying around like she’s got something on us.”

“She does…the facts. She knows who was driving that car and we didn’t have him. If we made a mistake in our identification, then we’re obligated to correct it. What else you got?”

“Blake is surveiling some fish company in Chelsea. Pete followed him there and they just sat outside watching the place until the early evening. Also, Blake had lunch with a big time Boston PI, named Morse and some Union Official.”

“Sounds like he’s got something on someone.”

“He might just be searching.”

“Are you alright? There’s got to be something you’re not telling.”

Billy let out a deep breath. “I’m not sure I can cut it. I mean…maybe, I’m not up to this anymore.”

“If you’re not, there’s no one else, here, who is. I know we haven’t covered a lot of hard news, but, trust me, you can handle this. Look at the way you’ve been going after City Hall on those land deals. In a small town, that's much more far-reaching than whatever Blake's got...more important, too."

"It doesn't seem like it."

"Well, you let me worry about that. You just do the job you've been trained to do and nail that story."

Billy looked at him and flashed a forced smile before turning his attention away. Self-doubt and pity were ugly attributes that Billy had long tried to bury, though every once in a while they got the better of him. He knew they would pass. He hoped it would be soon.

Fox watched him start to type, again, deciding to leave him and his demons alone.

In The Company of Thieves

It was already ten when Pete followed Blake to his vantage point in the lower stairwell of an old rat infested apartment building across the street from the Bonner Fish Company. Blake settled in with a pad of paper, a camera and a handheld tape recorder. Pete settled on the upper front stoop of the building next to Blake's with a thermos of hot coffee and his .45.

For the next two hours the parking lot in front of the Fish Company remained empty. There was nothing going on for the entire length of the pier, or so it seemed. A solitary boat was still tied up behind Bonner and except for a half submerged old tug and an old fishing boat pulled out of the water and up on pilings the entire waterfront was devoid of related activity.

The air was crisp, a little cold for April with a solid cloud cover and a stiff breeze coming off the water it seemed more like the end of February. Pete sat in the doorway feeling like a homeless man trying to stave off the elements. He could see Blake's breath and thought to himself that Blake was a lot more uncomfortable than he, working out of Los Angeles as he did.

As Pete sat there and tried to keep himself from getting too bored, a small sporty two-seater pulled into the Bonner lot. He looked at the car and, then down at Blake, where he could hear the sound of Blake's camera clicking away. The car came to a stop and an older man, wearing a black leather jacket, black leather boots and dark shades got out. He stepped out of the car and cautiously surveyed the area. Satisfied that he was alone he pulled a cellular phone from his jacket pocket which he dialed as he approached and eventually, entered the building.

Pete didn't recognize him, but thought he recognized the outfit…small time hood, big time punk. He watched for any movement from Blake, but there was none.

After a few more minutes, another car pulled up to the building. This time two men got out. The first was Pierce. He opened his door and walked around to the back, opening the trunk and taking out a small black leather case. When he shut the trunk, another man could be seen waiting for him at the front of the car. It was Arthur Cogent.

Again, the whirring sound of Blake's camera reached Pete's position. Pete had never read this morning's paper and when Billy had showed him the pictures on the front page, Pierce's face did not register. He sat and watched, wondering what role, if any, these men had in the scheme Billy laid out the night before.

Finally, a third car arrived, pulling into the lot and stopping at the farthest end of the building. One man got out and walked around to the back of the building, looking over the boat and examining the structure of the pier. He was a large man, six feet tall and easily over two hundred pounds. Pete stared for a while and realized he recognized Jimmy Ponce, a runner and sometimes bodyguard for a local wise guy named Pirrella. Satisfied with what he had seen, he walked back to the front of the building and entered.

For the next two hours there was no movement. Blake and Pete sat and watched and waited.

Solitary Confusion

It was close to noon before Fox felt it wise to approach Billy about his sudden change of mood. Billy had long since finished his column and Fox was as impressed as ever with his style and grasp of subject matter.

"You want to grab some lunch? Claire is going to run some errands, so I thought maybe you and I could talk."

Billy reluctantly agreed and the two of them left for Coda's Cafe. It was a short walk, the brisk air reminding Fox how much he loved this time of year. Billy hardly noticed, still immersed in his thoughts, his self-inflicted doubt.

Once at the Cafe, Fox took a booth at the rear of the restaurant hoping they could get through the meal without being noticed. Fox had been away a long time and had forgotten what it was like to live in a small town, to be well known, to know so many people in such a small place. The rear booth was hidden from the front door and that, by itself, made it an appealing location to conduct an interview.

After ordering their meals, Fox pressed Billy for a context within which to put his sudden change of heart.

"Are you ready to get back to the story, Bill?"

"If there is a story."

"You know damn well there's a story...a potentially big story."

Coffee was set down in front of the two men and they silently prepared their brews, each in their own way. Billy never looked Fox in the eye, but he knew he would have to either explain himself or snap out of it. Fox would not let up until he felt certain that he had all the facts.

"I know you were disappointed in the way I acted this morning, but this is getting to be a pretty tough task. It's been over twenty years since something like this has fallen into my lap and I feel like I'm leading us down a path that I can't control."

"You're a reporter. You're not supposed to have control over the big stories. They control you. If you try to impose your will on them, they'll rush right by you. Someone else will tell the tale and get the credit. You have to go with the story...feel it. This story is big. You and I both know it.

"Even if all we were reporting about was letting that perp go, we'd have a hell of a tale to tell. Now, if we find out who this guy is and why they let him go, then we'd have a blockbuster. Maybe not a national blockbuster, but one that sure would shake up this cranky old city."

Billy took a long sip from his coffee. "Exactly who do you think we're chasing?"

Fox had covered a lot of stories that had the same feel as this one, but he never felt as out of touch with the movers and shakers, the people who usually knew what was really going on behind those closed doors.

"It's not clear to me. But, I think you're the best person to answer that question."

"I gave it a lot of thought last night and all I could come up with is that I'm overreacting to a couple of small events and making them some big conspiracy."

Fox was starting to get annoyed. He wasn't used to feeling like a reporter's Father Confessor.

"Listen, Bill, you've got a lot of talent. I've seen the best and you're right there as far as having the tools. You've got instincts, you've the ability to think fast and put things in their proper perspective. You can write beautiful pictures with words...as good as I've ever seen. But you don't trust yourself. You're afraid of success and you use what happened twenty years ago to stop you from experiencing it. I don't know what to tell you, other than you can do this...You have to do this. You don't belong on this paper. You've got too much ability to be wasting your life feeling sorry for yourself over something you had no control of."

As Fox finished his speech, he felt the familiar vibration of his pager. He pulled it out of his pocket, looked at the number and realizing that he was unfamiliar with it, he showed it to Billy.

"That's the number for the Teacher's Lounge at the High School. It must be Alex."

He got up from the table, walked to the pay phone in the corner and called Alex. He got her, alone, in the Teacher's lounge during the period of time it takes for classes to get reorganized after lunch. She was in a hurry, but happy to hear from him.

"What's up?"

She told him that the account number had been traced by her friend and that the money was being deposited into Pierce's account from an account that originated in Virginia. The account belonged to the Justice Department. Billy got a chill when she said it. Now, it would be hard to convince himself, let alone Fox, that there was nothing sinister going on.

When he got back to the table, Fox had already plunked down the cash for their meal and was waiting for Billy so they could get back to the office.

"You might want to have a seat."

Fox sat back down. "What did she find out?"

Billy looked around and in a voice that was close to a whisper informed Fox. "Pierce gets his money from the Justice Department."

"Is she certain?'

"She wouldn't call me if she wasn't."

"That means he's an agent of some kind."

Billy interrupted his train of thought. "Or a baby-sitter. This smells like a witness relocation."

"You're right about that."

"I want to get in touch with Pete. He's out there following Blake."

Fox scratched his chin and stared towards the front of the restaurant. "Do you think Blake knows who Pierce is?"

"I don't think he cares. Pierce isn't part of his story. Pierce is connected to the break-in. He's not supposed to be here."

"He's a variable Blake wasn't counting on. Pierce is our mystery man's watchdog."

The Boat

Blake and Pete sat in the crisp air watching the outside of the building as the afternoon stretched on for what seemed like an eternity. Finally, around three, the front door opened and all four men exited, the last man slamming the door and bolting it.

They made their way to their cars and were off. There were no good-byes and no small talk as they left the scene. Each man got into his vehicle and peeled out of the lot, each heading back to town and out of sight.

Blake was up and out of his hiding place within minutes of the departures. He walked back towards his car, Pete following at a short distance. Pete hesitated, looking back at the building, then moved to follow Blake.

Blake got into his car and headed off in the general direction of the men who they had just seen leave. Pete assumed that since they had to walk almost three blocks to get to their cars that there was no way that they would be able to catch up to them. While they were making their way to the cars, he decided that he wanted to take a look around Bonner.

After Blake was safely out of sight, Pete drove back towards the center of Chelsea stopping at Rico's Twenty Four Hour Variety that posted a payphone sign. He went into the store and was struck by the scarcity of products on the shelves. He knew he was in a poor part of town, but was surprised that more staples were not available. All conversation had stopped when he entered and when he saw how the three men behind the counter watched him, he knew what the primary business of this convenience store really was.

Trying to stay cool, he nodded in their direction, glad that he was carrying, hoping he was overly cautious. He got to the phone and dialed Billy.

Back at the office, Fox was working the phone, trying to get a hold of someone in Washington that would be able and willing to confirm their suspicions about Pierce and his charge. Claire took Pete's call and informed him that Billy was up at the high school getting some information from Alex.

Pete thought about giving up on the idea of searching Bonner. It was getting dark and he wanted to make sure Billy didn't mind his giving up on tailing Blake to do it. Claire was waiting for a message, so Pete gave her the address of the Fish Company and told her to get the information to Billy because he would be waiting for him. He told her that he would give Billy a half hour to get there. After that he would be off.

As he put the phone down he noticed that the three men had separated and were standing in different parts of the store, eyes still fixed on Pete. They had left the way clear to the door, so he assumed they meant for him to use it, either on his own or their insistence. He smiled and walked to the door, noticing that the Everett paper was sitting on the end of the counter.

Glancing down at it, he noticed the two pictures and for the first time it clicked. Pierce was one of the men he had seen at the Fish Company earlier. He had a connection between Blake's story and both the break-in and the accident. While he was making the connection, the three men had moved again. Noticing that one of them had gone out back, he turned and walked out the door, to his car and off towards Bonner. In his rearview mirror he saw the third man come around from the back of the building holding a baseball bat just as he turned the corner.

Billy walked into the office not five minutes after Pete called. He had some more specific information about the trail of the cash from

Virginia through an offshore account and into Pierce's account. Claire gave him the message and after noting the time, Billy handed the paper Alex had given him to Fox. Billy took the keys to his car out of his pocket and set off to find his friend.

Billy pulled in back of Pete's car, parked about a block away from the building. Pete got out of the car and greeted him.

"I want to take a look around and I figured that you'd want to join me."

They started to walk towards the building, Pete looking around cautiously.

"What are we looking for?"

"Beats me, but there was lot of activity, here, today and I'd like to find out why."

"You know, Pete, this two bit company has pretty good looking financials. If I didn't know better, I'd think they had an entire fleet of ships."

They approached the building slowly. The front door was padlocked so they went around to the rear of the building. While the front had just two small windows, the rear had three large picture windows covering the entire rear wall, facing the harbor.

Through the windows they could see a mostly empty warehouse. There was no equipment, no machinery or bins within which you could process your daily catch. There were only two items visible; an old gray metal desk in the center of the warehouse and two long crates bearing the markings of the U. S. Army. Neither box looked like it was open and because the windows were covered with years of neglect, what was visible was not crystal clear.

Billy continued to stare inside while Pete turned his attention to the boat tied up at the rickety dock behind the warehouse. He walked over to the boat and cautiously stepped onto the deck. His first stop was the wheelhouse that was nothing more than a small cabin above the Spartan sleeping compartment below decks. There was a chart table opposite the wheel, above which was a radio and a radar readout screen. Under the table was a cabinet, inside of which was an unlocked metal box that contained various papers pertaining to ownership and insurance of the boat itself.

The ship was listed as being leased by Bonner from a company called Tours Services of Steamboat Key Florida. Pete stuffed the paper into his shirt pocket and looked for anything else that might be of interest to Billy. Examining a stack of papers he found several references to the boat being of Panamanian registry. Other than that, there was nothing else of interest so he closed the box and pushed it back into the cabinet. By the time he was done, Billy had joined him on the boat and was about to enter the wheelhouse when Pete met him at the door.

Pete handed him the paper, told him about the contents of the room and the registry of the ship. By the time Billy had read the ownership document Pete had moved past him and opened a hatch at the rear of the boat. Billy turned to follow. As he turned, he was struck by the complete absence of nets and rigging. The boat had radar and some storage lockers on the deck, but nothing that made it look like a commercial fishing vessel.

Meanwhile, Pete was looking down into the darkness of the hold. Billy walked over to him and the two of them climbed down. It was damp and smelled of musty wood, gasoline and oil. With a flashlight they could see that it was mostly empty. A tool chest was in the corner and some yellow rain gear was lying on top of it.

Over in the corner, Billy noticed some strange looking debris. He picked up a couple of pieces of burlap that had twigs and leaves. In the bad light he couldn't be sure, but the feel and smell was marijuana. Pete picked similar material at the other end of the hold, putting some of it in an envelope. Billy called to Pete to go topside and the two of them climbed back onto the deck.

It was getting dark and a red hue hung over the city across the harbor. A few thin wispy clouds gave tone and depth to the magnificent colors. The breeze had picked up, off the water, making it seem much too cool for an April evening. Billy pulled the collar of his jacket up around his ears as he waited for Pete.

“Pete, where’s the fish odor?”

“I don’t know. Nothing about this boat says fishing to me.”

“I assume you saw the weed.”

Pete took out the envelope and showed it to him. “I figure Al can get this tested.”

“That’s the first hard evidence we’ve got that confirms Blake’s story.”

“I don’t like him, Scoop. But, my guess is that he was playing straight with you.”

Billy agreed, but he had the gnawing feeling that something wasn’t right. Blake wasn’t the kind of guy who would share information like that. It occurred to him that Blake might want him to play part of his hand. That maybe he was trying to shake someone out from under a rock or had reached a dead-end that Billy might be able to stumble through.

Whatever Blake's motives, it was too late to back off and too damn interesting to drop.

Pushing the Accelerator

Once away from the boat they split up. Billy had to go back to the office and Pete had promised Alex a bite to eat. As Billy got into his car he took a long look back at the Bonner Fish Company, then drove away through the empty streets, back towards Everett. By the time Billy made it out of the waterfront district, Pete was long gone. The quickest route out of Chelsea took Billy down a series of back streets behind junkyards, warehouses, recycling companies and the rear of the area's largest produce market.

Within a few minutes he had reached the Parkway that separated the two cities. As fate would have it, he was half a block from the storage facility where Pierce had his locker. He made a mental note and drove across a busy intersection and into Everett, behind the main drag leading to the Square. He was preoccupied with attempting to put the recent events into some useful context when the blue Cresseda pulled in behind him.

As he turned off Broadway there was little room between the two cars. A short trip down a residential street would take Billy to the newspaper, but as he made the last turn onto Liberty Street, the car behind him sped up and smacked his car's bumper, throwing Billy forward and into a state of confusion. He looked into the rear mirror and through the darkened glass could not see the driver.

The first jolt took him to the edge of the curb. He decided not to wait for the next one. He put his foot hard down on the accelerator and sped down the street, hoping there would be no pedestrians. He literally flew past the newspaper office and cut the corner in front of it short on two wheels. The Cresseda followed and accelerated to match his speed. Billy would attempt to lead the unknown assailant right to the police station, but it was a long way off.

Billy was usually a cautious driver, but he had great confidence in his ability to handle any road condition or situation. This was not one he had encountered before. He was clear of the pursuer by a half block, but knew he wouldn't be able to hold that lead for long. He tried to think of streets that he could take and still keep up his speed without endangering anyone. That was no easy task as Everett was an old, largely residential city and most of the streets were narrow and packed with two and three story homes.

Even Broadway was barely able to handle two lanes of traffic with parking on both sides. The bright spot was that if he could make it to Broadway there was a greater chance that the pursuit might break off or that a police car would see what was going on and intervene. Broadway, however, was still a couple of long streets away and he had chosen a long straight street from which to try and outrun his pursuer. The lead was evaporating quickly. He kept his foot to the floor, trying to keep an eye on the road and one on his attacker. He kept his palm on his horn, as much to scare off any foot traffic as to attract attention.

Too late! The street was too long and the Cresseda had too much speed. The impact was brutal and sustained forcing Billy to loose control, careening off a tree and into the rear of a parked car. Billy jammed his right shoulder into the steering wheel preventing himself from being thrown into the windshield. The car came to a sudden stop halfway into the trunk of an old beat up Taurus. Glass shattered, horns engaged, steam erupted from under his hood.

Billy quickly turned towards the other car, expecting another run. The Cresseda sat in the middle of the street for a long moment, seemingly suspended in time. Billy saw the passenger side window roll down, but could only make out the shape of a man's head behind the wheel. Billy pushed on his door and extricated himself from the wreck, just as the attacker sped away, hitting the top of Hancock Street and screeching it's way around the corner and out of sight.

The street was rapidly filling with people, several of whom had come running over to Billy to offer assistance. He was standing by his pile of junk staring in disbelief as the Cresseda disappeared. When the first person arrived, he asked them to call the police and ask for Al. Then he started asking if anyone had seen the license plate of the vehicle. No one had. Billy walked over to the curb and sat down.

Within two or three minutes, he could hear the sirens and for the first time noticed that his shoulder was starting to ache; a dull throb slowly expanding into a sharp searing pain. Looking up, he saw Al running towards him, one hand on his baton, the other holding a speaker into which he was screaming for an ambulance and some more back up.

Chapter Seven

A Side of Solace and Desert

Pete and Alex were sitting in a booth at Coda's, having a cup of coffee, waiting for their dinner and staring out at the Square that was relatively empty for early evening. Pete was busy explaining how exhilarated he felt after his run-in with the "druggies" and the search of the boat. He told Alex just how much he enjoyed being in the thick of something big. She marveled at his boyish enthusiasm, something that had been missing for a long time.

Their relationship went back a long way. While Pete and Billy had been close friends, even before High School, Alex hadn't caught up with them until their senior year. She was a couple of years younger and knew the two of them through an older brother that used to hang around with Pete. From afar she had always admired him and, truth be told, had had a schoolgirl crush since she was in Junior High School.

Pete never noticed her much and it wasn't until a party that senior year that he even started talking to her. She had known Billy a bit longer, both having been in an honor's writing program. She thought back to those days, now, and remembers thinking that Billy was a bit full of himself, too confident, too certain that things would turn out a certain way. Of course, Billy was with Terry and a relationship with him was never even imagined. But, Pete was another story.

They hit it off immediately and, even though, Pete thought of her as a little girl, he was finding her company more and more fun as the year went on. They started to hang on weekends and some evenings, Billy, Terry, Al and a couple of brainiacs making up the rest of their crew. As always happens at the end of senior year they split up, went their separate ways.

Billy and Terry went off to school. Pete turning down an opportunity to attend a local school in favor of hanging around, aggravating his parents and generally doing anything his father warned him not to do. Alex, of course, was still in school so she was around all the time for him to confide in and keep company. Alex was never very good at pursuing men, so she never let on that she wanted more out of their relationship. Pete never picked it up, or if he did, he never let on.

By the next Christmas, they were very close. However, by that same time, Pete's father, one of the few truly wealthy men in the city, started making noise about putting Pete to work or moving out of the house. Pete's father owned a food processing business and Pete was no more interested in that, than he was in college. So, he joined the Marines.

This move broke Alex's heart and created a rift between he and his father that was never fully bridged. Once Pete got into the service, he started to develop some skills and his father actually felt a pang of pride at Pete's being chosen for special schooling. However, the pride was short-lived as, after Pete was put on active duty in Vietnam, he was abruptly court marshaled and terminated from active service. Pete came home and refused to discuss the circumstances surrounding his dismissal, further alienating his dad and making it difficult for Alex to penetrate the new protective barriers he had erected.

Now, once again, they sat in a restaurant talking about him and Billy and, once again, she kept her feelings buried. Their meals were finally delivered and they had begun to eat, when Pete spotted Al and Billy entering. Alex saw the sling first and got up and ran over to him.

"What on earth happened?"

Alex, Al and Billy walked to the table where Pete helped get Billy situated. Billy had a little smile on his face as he shook his head at Alex's fawning.

"So, are you going to tell us?" Pete wanted to know.

"Not much to tell. After we split up, I headed back to the office when some car must've followed me. On Liberty they bumped me towards the curb, but I was able to keep control. I figured I'd try to outrun them and headed for police headquarters. I really didn't get too far. Just before I got to the top of Linden, they forced me into a tree and then a parked car."

Alex wanted to know about the sling.

"Just a precaution. I jammed it into the steering wheel when I hit the car. It all happened so fast..."

"Who did it?"

Al interrupted. "I think that's got to be obvious. Our mystery man thinks you guys are getting too close to something."

"All I really want to know, is who is this SOB? That's all. I don't give a rat's ass about what they're smuggling in through Chelsea. I just got to find out who this guy is." Billy had a lot more conviction in his voice than he did this morning.

"What about smuggling?" Asked a curious Al.

Pete jumped in. "I've been tailing Blake, who's been staking out some fish company on the Chelsea waterfront. Earlier today, Billy and I went over there and took a good look at a boat they got tied up to the dock in back."

He reached into his coat pocket and handed Al the envelope of powder and leaves he had taken from the boat. "What do you make of this?"

Al reached into the bag and felt the substance inside, then brought the envelope to his nose and sniffed.

"It's pot. Where'd you get it?"

"It's all over the cargo hold of that boat. We figure it's what Blake has been looking into. I saw some lowlifes over there, today. They didn't look much like fishermen to me."

Al was concerned. "Hey, you watch yourself over there. I don't have much influence with the Chelsea Police, so if you get into trouble, I won't be much help."

"I don't think we'll be snooping around there, for a while at least. But I got to tell you, I'm going back there when Blake does."

In the meantime Alex had been massaging the back on Billy's neck and he was arching his back to get the full impact of her technique. The waitress came over and Billy ordered just a cup of coffee. Al wanted nothing.

Pete looked at Al as angry as Al had ever remembered seeing him. "I heard your boss nixed the idea of protection for our man, here. You think he's smart enough to see things more clearly now, or would you like me to explain it to him?"

"I think the last thing any of us need, right now, is for you to do any grandstanding. Leave Roselli to me. I keep telling you he's a stand up guy. He'll change his mind…trust me.

Billy, you okay? I got to get back and file a report."

Billy nodded, but Alex jumped in. "What about tonight, Al. Don't you think they might come back to finish the job."

"First, I think they completed the job. They just wanted to scare him off. And secondly, Pete, here, is the man for the job tonight. I'll have a car outside your building, but I think Pete should plan on spending the night."

Pete and Alex were in agreement. In fact, Alex wanted to stay, as well. Both Pete and Billy knew enough not to argue the point, so after they finished downing their meals and a quick cup of coffee they headed for Billy's place. Since it was a couple of blocks down the street, Pete decided to leave his car in the municipal lot and the three walked out of Coda's and into the evening air.

Billy wanted something a little stronger than common aspirin, so they stopped at the 24-hour convenience store on the way. Pete picked up a six-pack, but Alex assured him that he would not be drinking any of it. After the store, they walked through the Square and over to Billy's building. They entered the lobby, Billy entering his pass code as Pete searched the street for any suspicious vehicles, half expecting to find one with a dent in the front matching the damage to Billy's car.

Soon they were in Billy's apartment. Alex made a pot of coffee and Billy and Pete compared notes in the Living room. Alex set the cups down on the coffee table and told them who was going to sleep where. Neither, Billy or Pete objected, having learned long ago that Alex was a woman who liked to be in charge, made sound decisions and generally had a better grasp of what was going on than they did.

As it was only seven thirty, they decided to sort through the details of what they had before going to bed. The room had two couches, a sofa and a love seat. Alex would take the longer couch and Pete would curl up on the love seat. She had insisted that Billy sleep in his own bed and politely turned down his slightly, tongue-in-cheek offer to share his king sized bed.

But for now, the three friends sat and stared at one another, a little nervous, a little excited. Billy felt strange. After a night of soul searching that led him to conclude that he couldn't handle the story, he was surprised that his feelings had changed so thoroughly after the accident. The accident convinced him that he wasn't afraid of the physical dangers, at least not for himself, but that he was afraid of letting everyone down. It all came back to the same thing; if he didn't write the story, then he couldn't fail to do it right.

By eleven o'clock, Billy was ready for bed. He was drowsy from the medication and spent from the discussion of various scenarios that they had bounced around the room. Alex was clearing away the cups and telling Pete that he had better get used to the idea that they would be shutting the lights soon. Pete was staring out the sliders grumbling about being ordered around.

Billy was heading for his room, Alex to the bathroom and Pete for a beer, when the buzzer from downstairs sounded. They all froze, looking at one another as if deer caught in oncoming headlights. Then Pete reminded them that it would be highly unlikely that a killer would announce his arrival. Pete answered and it was Fox. He wanted to come up.

Pete opened the door and waited for the elevator to arrive. It was only a couple of minutes before Fox was seated on the couch asking how

Billy was feeling and telling them that he had gotten a call from Roselli telling him about the incident and guaranteeing that there would be someone watching Billy from now on.

Alex was the most relieved, Pete the most skeptical. Billy thanked Fox for coming over and offered him something to drink or eat. Fox settled for one of Pete's beers. Then he told them why he had really come over.

"I wanted to talk to you anyway. I've spent a great deal of time on the phone to Washington. It appears that we may have stumbled into something a lot more serious than a Federal witness. I couldn't get any information on who our hostage taker is, other than extremely dangerous. But this guy Pierce, he's one for the books. He's a career screw-up. He's been reassigned several times over the years, messing up one assignment after another.

My friend at Justice says that he's on his way to forced retirement soon and that the speculation is that he got some very important friends or he would've been out a long time ago. Did you ever hear of a US Embassy liaison in Mexico City, misidentifying Lee Harvey Oswald back in '63? Well, that was our boy, Pierce. His first assignment, even reiterated his story before the Warren Commission, even though the pictures clearly showed two men of different heights, weights and build."

"He could've lied on purpose. Isn't that the most accepted version?" Billy was very familiar with most of the JFK assassination stories, myths and plots.

"Maybe. Anyway, my man is a little concerned about Pierce. It seems he requested this Baby-sitting job and has been manipulating Justice to move this guy all around the country. They want to pull the plug and bring both of them back to Washington. Your stories got a lot of attention. I think they know they've been taken for a ride."

With that Fox got up and walked to the door. He assured Billy that if he needed to take some time off to recover that the story would still be waiting when he got back.

"That's a nice sentiment, I'm sure Claire will be happy that you made the offer, but you know I've got to be there tomorrow. Trust me I'm fine. Tell her not to worry…I got Alex, here, to do that."

With that Fox laughed as he exited and the three friends sat back down on the couch for more speculation. It would be close to three by the time they all went to bed.

Ghost Writer

The sun was starting to show on the horizon, gradually lighting the skies above in that purple glow that accompanies the dawn. It was just after six and Roselli was walking along the shoreline of Revere Beach as was his custom once the weather turned decent again. The coast had a natural curvature, here, that made it the perfect site for a beach.

Shortly after the turn of the century it became one of the first such recreational sites in the United States. For decades it was the place to be, where generations of young men and women came to play in the summer sun and experience the pains of maturity in the sweltering heat of the humid summer nights.

Until the late sixties it was bordered by a large amusement park that stretched half the length of the beach that was almost two miles. The far end was covered with small beach cottages and some larger year-round homes. But by the end of the sixties it had all fallen into disrepair as the advent of the booming fifties economy and the access to Cape Cod took away the vacationers, leaving just the daily beach crowd and an evermore sleazy night element to dominate the scene.

Now, all the honky-tonks, rides, pizza parlors and sandwich shops had all been torn down, replaced by enormous condominiums and grassy parks. The small summer cottages had all been converted into small, overpriced homes. The beach had been cleaned up, too and it was common to find dozens of health inspired strollers and joggers roaming the beach every morning. Roselli was one of them. No matter what the weather, you would find him here every morning by five thirty. By six thirty he was having a light breakfast and by seven he was at the police gym working himself into a lather. After a quick shower, he was at his desk, promptly at eight.

Today, Roselli was lost in his thoughts. He hadn't had a good night's sleep and was more convinced than ever, that trouble had come to Everett. The night before, he was preparing to go to the track, when he got Al's call about the attack on Billy. Upset by his own lack of foresight he tried to get a hold of Billy to apologize, but was unsuccessful. He did speak with Fox, assuring him that Billy would be protected and that this situation would be getting more attention from his Department.

By the time he left for the track it was almost eight. No daily double, though gambling was far from his mind as he showed up to meet with the guys. Cogent was up at the window when he got there. Holland and Blair were nursing their loses.

Gil Holland saw him first. "Well if it isn't Cappy. What's shakin'?"

Roselli sat down and stared out at the track, then turned to his friends. "Anything hot, tonight?"

"Not a thing." stated Blair. "Arthur's the only one to cash so far."

"Good. Dinner's on him."

They all laughed at Roselli's joke, more out of consideration, than pure comedic touch.

"What's so funny?" Asked Cogent, standing by his chair putting his winnings into a pocket before sitting down.

"The captain, here, thinks you should pay for diner. Come on splurge for a change." Holland figured a little ribbing would be good for him, he was so serious most of the time.

"I suppose. I just picked up a little scratch, so I can afford to be magnanimous." He looked over at Roselli and smiled. Then he turned to a waitress walking nearby and asked that she take their dinner orders. She was a bit taken aback by his abrupt manner but made her way over to the table, pen and pad in hand. They all ordered sandwiches and drinks, the last to order being Cogent who dismissed the poor woman with the wave of his hand.

As usual the conversation centered on the events of the day; politics, mainly, national and international. Roselli was more keenly aware of the cynical slant Cogent placed on everything they discussed. According to him, people, places and events were never what they seemed. He had once said that history was just the spin those in power placed on events; the truth seldom working its way onto the written page. Every treaty was a back room deal. Every war a conspiratorial exercise in the production of wealth.

By the time they had finished their meal, Holland and Blair were laughing at his proclamation that only those who lived their lives in the shadows were privy to the truth. He exclaimed that they should be the ones to write the history books, not idealistic scholars or sentimental buffoons. Roselli wasn't laughing.

Towards the end of the evening, Holland got up to cash in a couple of small wins. Blair was getting tired, his head bouncing off his chest as he tried to listen to them talk and watch the last few races. Roselli saw an opportunity.

"Arthur, I'd like to have a talk with you. I suggest we take a walk."

Cogent studied him for a moment, concluding he was serious and deciding to go along with him. They told Blair that they were going downstairs and that they would be back shortly. Roselli led the way as they climbed down the stairs and out the doors onto to the paved area bordering the stretch where most of the true bettors stood to watch their picks cross the finish line.

It was a cool night and Arthur wasn't prepared for the drastic change in temperature. He wanted to expedite matters. "What's on your mind, Captain?"

"I want to know what you know."

"About?"

"I want to know if you know who I had locked up." Roselli had inched right up to his face.

"Be careful how you say things, my friend. I'm not used to being interrogated."

"Just what are you used to?"

"For that, you'll have to read my memoirs. I'm sure you'll find the reading very interesting."

"You pompous ass. I should've guessed you'd try to rewrite history. What publisher would print your version of the truth."

"Never you mind that. I've got it all worked out. Once I'm dead, the book will be published: "A Life in the Shadows" by someone who lived there."

"Enough of your delusions! What do you know about what's going on?"

"Not as much as you obviously think. I'm retired, remember?"

Roselli looked away and shook his head. Cogent continued to look at him with a bemused, studying stare.

"I can tell you two things. First, your man is an independent operator. I don't know who he is or who hired him or why, for that matter. But Blake Flatly makes a lot of enemies. In fact, the second thing I can tell you is that if Flatly continues to dig, he's going to wind up dead. You can take that to the bank."

"Who?"

"Don't know. But my sources tell me that he's making a lot of very powerful men very angry."

"They have a hit out on him? I've already got one attempted murder. I don't want another."

"Attempted murder?" Cogent was honestly surprised.

"Yeh, someone forced a local newsman into a parked car earlier this evening."

"Oh, that. I heard about it on my police radio. It seems to me that was hardly attempted murder. If they wanted kill him they would have. I think they were just making a point."

"Maybe."

Cogent started to go back upstairs, when Roselli had just one more question for him.

"Arthur, could you find out who this guy is, if you wanted to?"

He turned back with that smug smile firmly planted on his lips.

"If I wanted. But it better be quick, because I've decided to help a couple of friends with a project they have going, so I won't be around as much. At least for a while."

"What do you need?"

"Get me a picture and I'll FAX it to DC. I'm not making any promises, but if he's a real pro, they should have something on him."

With that he turned and walked up the stairs, shouting back; "Good night, Captain. You know where to reach me."

Roselli watched him leave and then made his way to the exit and a long sleepless night. He tossed ideas around in his head till dawn, but nothing was any clearer. Now, at the beach, he was trying to clear his mind so that he could tackle it all again. He bent down and picked up a few stones, throwing them into the surf, before turning towards the street, deciding he had had enough of this mindless meandering for one morning. It was time to get more actively involved…

Road to Recovery

In spite of the late hour at which they went to sleep, Billy and Alex were awake and scurrying around the apartment by six thirty. Pete slept in his chair clutching a pillow as Billy put on the coffee while Alex quickly washed. She was in the bigger rush, since she had to go back to her place, shower, change into some fresh clothes and still get to school by eight. Just in case, today was a good day to be late since her first period was a study hall.

She splashed cold water on her face and rushed back into the kitchen, grabbing a hot cup of coffee from Billy as he passed her on his way to the bathroom. Pete continued to sleep, oblivious to the rush of people around him.

By the time Billy was done in the bathroom, Alex was done with her coffee and was ready to head out. Billy thanked her for her concern and gave her a peck on the cheek. She reminded Billy to put the sling on and take it easy for a day or so. He lied and said he would. She knew he lied and smiled at him. Before leaving she walked over to Pete and lightly kissed him on the forehead. He didn't move so she shrugged her shoulders and walked towards the door, saying; "I don't know why I try."

"Yes, you do." Was all Billy said in reply. He opened the door and she was gone, down the hall and off to work. Billy watched until she was on the elevator, then he turned and went back inside. He walked over to Pete and roughly shook his shoulders. Pete stirred enough to open one eye. There was a look of confusion, then revelation on his face as he realized where he was.

"What time is it?"

"It's a little after seven. Come on, I got to get to the office."

"Where's Alex?"

"She's gone. She had to go home."

Billy was pouring a cup of coffee for Pete who was slowly getting to his feet and stretching.

"No good-bye? How uncool."

"She tried, but you wouldn't budge. Now get your ass over here and have a bite before I have to leave too."

Pete made his way to the table in short shuffling steps. He was rubbing his back the whole time.

"I've slept in more comfortable places."

Billy placed a bowl and a box of cereal in front of him.

"You call that breakfast?"

"No, I call it a fast breakfast. Now, have some so we can take off."

"Why don't you just leave me, here? I can fend for myself."

"And eat me out of house and home? I don't think so."

Pete laughed, took a long appreciative sip from his mug and grabbed the box from Billy.

"What are we up to today?" Pete wanted to know.

"I'm gonna try to get Fox to contact some of his old Washington contacts and see if they can find who this guy is and just exactly who is paying Pierce 6 grand a month to watch him."

"You want me to keep following Blake, I assume."

"Yup and you want to get some pictures, today?"

"No problem."

Billy and Pete finished eating. Billy put everything away while Pete ran off to the bathroom. Ten minutes later they were heading out the door. In the elevator they discussed Pierce's background, Pete wondering how a guy goes from embassy spy to baby-sitter. He reasoned that if he were such a screw up he would no longer be employed. The two possibilities left them with a choice between his pissing someone off or his baby-sitting someone important. Both of them were afraid of the latter.

As they exited the building they walked through the square and straight for Pete's car. They were too engrossed in their conversation to notice two men sitting in a parked car across from Billy's. The two men were Pierce and Hoffman Muir.

"I don't suppose there's anything inside we need to see, is there?" asked Pierce.

Hoffman just shook his head, never taking his eyes off the two of them as they moved further and further away.

"Shouldn't we follow them?" Pierce was tired of always having to wait for a response from Muir, always having to be his own company. He had known Muir for almost thirty years, though like most people who ran in these circles, he too believed Muir had been killed in the early eighties by the Iranian Secret Police. And like most he was stunned when he suddenly appeared out of nowhere a little over a year ago, needing a cover from which to pursue some old unfinished business. And what better cover than the Witness Relocation Program.

"If we're not going to follow them, then why the hell have we been sitting here for the last three hours?"

"You talk too much. Let's go, I'll tell you where, when I know."

Pierce saw the look in his eyes and decided to start the car and drive away from Billy and Pete.

*****

Billy reached the office just after seven thirty. Fox and Claire were already working, though Claire stopped what she was doing and ran over to Billy to give him a motherly hug and tell him how he should probably be resting. As Billy was no longer wearing the splint she had no idea that he had suffered a slight shoulder sprain. Billy knew that if she caught wind of that he would be fighting off her motherly instincts all day and that was something he wasn't prepared to endure.

He politely acknowledged her concern and then sat at his desk. From a jacket pocket he pulled out a few notes that he had written the night before. He was dying to speak with Fox about their conjecture regarding Pierce, but before he could do that he wanted to see if there was anything that Fox might have said that would shed additional light on the subject.

While he was scanning his notes, the phone rang and Fox answered it. It was a short conversation and when Fox hung up he was a bit perplexed. He walked over to Billy and informed him that Roselli had requested that the two of them take a ride over to see him.

"It doesn't sound sinister. He couldn't have been nicer."

Billy thought for a moment. "Maybe, he wants something."

"Well, he probably wants to know where we are with our investigation." Fox had been through this before. A friendly call from the local constabulary as a pretense to more forceful questioning once on the inquisitor's home turf. "We should be very cautious, I think."

"When does he want to see us?"

"At our convenience. I suppose he'll want to apologize for nixing the protection Al promised you. Beyond that, who knows?"

"You know I haven't seen any police, today, either. I wonder what's up with that."

"Well, he said he'd send a car if we wanted one. Do we?"

"I don't know about you, but I've got no interest in driving through the city streets in the back seat of a squad car."

"Quite right. Besides, if we go on our own, he won't have the chance to prepare for us."

Billy hadn't taken off his jacket, so he looked at Fox and asked if he felt like going over there, now. Fox told him it was up to him. Billy was anxious to get back to work, so he told Fox that now was as good a time as ever. Fox grabbed his coat and they were off.

The city traffic was heavy as it was approaching the beginning of school and the maddening morning commute. Everett was just on the other side of the Mystic River from Boston, so it was a convenient place to live for those who worked in the city and it was a shortcut for those who lived a little further away. Fox maneuvered his way down Broadway, against the heaviest traffic flow and onto Ferry Street to the new Police building just off Ferry on Elm Street.

He pulled into the lot and noticed, that from all outward appearances it was a quiet day for the Everett Police Department. They had their choice of spaces and parked as close to the building as possible. Fox asked Billy if he was ready and Billy replied that he thought this was a good opportunity to gather more information. Fox tempered his own enthusiasm by telling Billy that this might simply be an apology for denying Al's request for protection.

Billy got out, turned to Fox and told him that he didn't think Roselli would waste everyone's time for something so trivial. Fox shrugged. He was thinking along the same lines as they walked towards the building. Entering they noticed how calm everything seemed. There were a couple of officers behind the glass-enclosed front desk, monitoring traffic and answering phone calls. Two uniformed officers walked past them joking about some personal matter.

Heading upstairs to the detective's squad room, they saw no one. Billy was expecting to see men scurrying around, hinting at the expected volcano waiting to erupt. As they reached the top landing they could see Roselli in his office at the far end, head down, busily writing on some unseen papers. They were cautious as they approached. Fox had had no dealings with

Roselli, so he didn't know what to expect. Billy just wanted to be somewhere else.

Roselli looked up as they reached his waiting area, rose from his desk and with an engaging smile came to the door to meet them. The smile was disarming to them both. They were ushered into his office sitting opposite his desk. Roselli sat down and asked if they wanted anything to drink, both abstained.

Roselli gathered his thoughts, then; "I know you want to know why I wanted to talk with you. It's nothing nefarious. I just want to know where you are in your investigation."

"Why? Haven't you been looking into this on your own?" Billy wasn't surprised.

"According to policy, there's nothing to investigate."

"I can't imagine that you've just ignored it."

"I haven't ignored it, but there is nothing of an official nature I can do. That's why I'd like to know if you have any idea who this guy is."

Fox, who had been listening quietly, shifted in his seat and placed a hand on Billy's shoulder to get his attention. Billy turned towards him as; "Captain, you know what we know since we've been reporting everything since it happened. Do you have any theories you might want to share with us?"

Roselli leaned forward. "I've got some questions, but no real theories. I'm hoping we're working on the same side of this thing. It galls me to think we had to release a piece of scum simply because someone got a phone call."

"Do you have any idea why a phone call was made on his behalf?" Fox wanted Roselli to do most of the talking.

"Listen, we all think this guy was in the witness protection program. That's got to be the most obvious answer. But that doesn't tell me who he is."

"Why do you need to know who if you know what he is?" Asked Fox.

"Let's just say that I think there is more here than meets the eye."

"Let's get down to cases. What do you want from us, aside from the guy's identity…which we don't know, by the way." Billy decided that the sparring was useless and that there might be something here for both of them. He was certain that Fox had already figured that out.

"What's really going on Cap'?" Fox knew from past experience that men like Roselli always knew more than they were willing to tell, but that coaxed, they might tell enough to clearly see from where they were coming.

"My gut tells me that this guy is big. I've had some contact with a guy who is supposed to be retired CIA and I get the feeling that he knows quite a bit. He tells me he doesn't know who the guy is, but I get the feeling his friends in Washington sure do."

"Tell him, Bill." Fox wanted to get their cards on the table.

"We think he's a murderer."

"What! You didn't think that was important enough for me to know?"

"It gets worse. We don't know if he's involved, but there's something going down that involves smuggling stolen military hardware for drugs."

"Proof?"

"Nothing concrete, but the fingerprints are there and we've seen the remnants of one of the drug shipments, over in the Chelsea harbor. Pete found it."

"He's involved, too?"

"You didn't expect otherwise, did you?" Billy asked sarcastically.

"I suppose not." He paused, as he gauged his next response. "Why murder and not the smuggling?"

"It could be both, but I can't connect him to the people involved, directly. However, I suspect that he broke into Blake's room to either find out what he knew of the operation or to stop him from telling anyone else."

"And murder?" Roselli wanted all the facts so he could make up his own mind.

"Well that's pretty thin too, but there have been a couple of murders that have occurred around the smuggling operations. We're guessing right now that they're related. They occurred either in buildings owned by the people most closely associated with the smuggling or right around their properties."

"But why him? What proof do you have that he's a killer?"

"None, yet." Billy was a bit disturbed.

"You have a story, but you've got squat. We don't know if he's the one who tried to run you off the road."

"No, we don't. That's why we haven't come to you or printed any of this in the papers."

Fox was tired of the questions, though he knew everything the captain said was true. They had no proof; a lot of suspicions, but no hard, tangible proof that their man was a killer. Fox had one piece of information that he had yet to tell Billy that suddenly seemed more important.

"We do have one piece of good circumstantial evidence." Billy was caught off guard by Fox's remarks but was interested to find out what he was going to tell Roselli. "I spoke with a friend at the Justice Department. He doesn't know who this guy is, but he's been tracking Pierce and he was in both New Orleans and the Florida Keys at the time of the two murders."

"That makes Pierce a suspect, not this other guy."

"Pierce is his watchdog." Then he turned to Billy; "I didn't mean to hold that back, but we ran out of the office so fast that I didn't get the chance."

Billy had already surmised that both men had been in New Orleans and Florida. Having confirmation helped reinforce his rebounding confidence and justified his getting the others involved.

Roselli sat still for a couple of minutes digesting the thin threads of a story Billy and Fox were spinning. He wasn't sure they had enough to make a charge of murder, but he believed it all made sense.

"There was another reason I asked you, here. It's related, but I'm not sure how, just yet. My retired CIA acquaintance claims to have written a book that won't be published until after his death. He says it's a tell-all with some scary stuff."

Fox had an idea where he was going with this, but didn't interrupt.

"I figured one of you might have some contacts that could locate this book in advance of his death. My gut tells me it's tied into this whole affair."

Fox thought for a moment. "Without knowing the publisher or who his literary agent is, it's impossible."

"That's what I was afraid you'd say. Well, if you have any ideas, let me know. The name of the book is; 'A Life in the Shadows.' It's by an Arthur Cogent." After he said that he stood and walked over to the windows.

"I've got to tell you, I don't like the idea of a murderer operating with impunity in my city." Then he turned towards them; "I want him."

Chapter Eight

Donuts & Information

Pete had fumbled with his keys after watching Billy walk through the parking lot to the newspaper office. He wasn't used to being awake this early unless he was just getting home. He sat in his car staring up at the sun and shaking his head, trying to clear it enough to drive. His first thought was to head home and go back to sleep, until realizing he had promised to let Al know how Billy was doing.

Checking the clock tower that rose above the square on the Universalist Church he noted that it was still early enough to catch Al before his shift started. He started the car and drove towards the far end of town using only back streets to avoid the morning traffic crush. His theory was to either sleep through Rush Hour all together or stay on the back roads to avoid the logjams and bumper-to-bumper encounters that so often set him off.

After a little fancy maneuvering; an illegal turn or two, a quick corner through a gas station and a wrong way trip down one of the many one-way streets; he pulled into the Donut Maker across from Pope John High School. It was filled with teens hurrying to catch that first bell while stuffing themselves with donuts, muffins, pastries or bagels. Off in the corner, he spotted Al, in uniform drinking a coffee and dunking a plain cruller. A tall young man of slight build, shaved pate and wide smile sat opposite him.

Pete couldn't believe he hadn't seen Al, Jr. in such a long time that it didn't occur to him that he was almost a grown man. He stared and recalled that he and Al were close to that same age when they first started to hang together. It seemed like such a long, lifetime ago. Al, Jr. finished a soda and the last remnants of a pastry, wiped his hands and mouth, grabbed his backpack and rose from the table. He gave his old man a little tap on the shoulder and he was off to class. He walked right by Pete without a notice as he tried to catch up with a friend or two already out the door.

Pete saw the pride and affection on Al's face as a quick thought about the simple perfection of a father and son having breakfast before school passed through his, suddenly, clear brain. He used to make fun of Al being a father. Now, that seemed so childish.

Al hadn't noticed him, so Pete went to the counter and grabbed a cup of coffee and a couple of filled donuts before sitting down across from him. Al was surprised to see him, considering that the only times he had seen him this early, he was usually drunk or unconscious.

"What's shakin', Papa?"

"Did you see Little Al?"

"Saw him and noticed that he still has his mother's good looks, thank God."

"Yeh, yeh. So, tell me, how's Billy doing?"

"Alex and I stayed the night. He's back on his feet."

"He went to work, didn't he?" Al was exasperated.

"You expected him to stay home?"

"I suppose not. But he can't be running all over the place, if he expects us to protect him."

Pete finished wolfing the first donut; Al amazed at the raw energy expended to devour it. He wiped his mouth, then looked up at Al.

"I didn't see any of your guys this morning, by the way. Are they that good or did Roselli renig?"

"They'll be at the paper all day. Right outside. We want visibility."

The two men finished their coffee; Pete devouring another donut to complete his meal. Al informed Pete that it was time he checked in.

"I got to get going, my shift starts in fifteen. You keep me posted if anything new happens."

"Relax, Billy and I won't be foraging around any more fishing boats for a while."

"Is there anything you want me to do?"

"I don't know. Did your lab boys analyze the weed?"

"Yeh, it was pot. By the way, are you going over to the Chelsea waterfront?"

"I'm tailing Blake. That's where I'm headed, now. We know there's something up...and, it's big. Stay tuned."

The two of them got up at the same time and walked to the door, off to their morning duties.

"You stay well. I don't need anything else to worry about."

Pete laughed. "Aren't I always careful?" Then he walked towards his car, looking over his shoulder.

"Now, I'm really worried." Al was starting to talk to himself.

His Next Move

The Chelsea waterfront was mostly quiet. Even with the tide, there was little activity; a pleasure craft heading out of Admiral's Bay Marina towards the open channel, a coal barge being towed past the decaying piers en route to the power plant in Everett and a small tug grinding to a halt a couple hundred yards offshore waiting to assist in guiding a large container ship from it's berth in Charlestown, across the harbor.

The morning air was cool and heavy, smelling of diesel fuel and raw sewage that lined the inner harbor. Inside the Bonner Fish Company, streaks of sunlight glowed through the broken skylight and through open rusted seams in the roof and sides facing the harbor. The office was barren; a table and four or five folding chairs against one wall, an old metal desk, filing cabinet and broken chair against the exterior wall facing the street. A window of glass and chicken wire, stained by a film of rust, grime and salt air was above the desk.

Hoffman Muir stared out the window. Dominic Pierce sat on a folding chair, feet propped on the desk leafing through a yellowing newspaper that had been on top of the old unused file cabinet.

"What are we doing, here, Hoffman?" He put the paper on top of the desk, got up and walked over to the window. Muir didn't move a muscle continuing to stare at the figure seated in the shadows of an open doorway across the street. Looking over his shoulder, Pierce managed a small line of sight, but could make out very little.

"How can you see anything through that filth?" Muir remained still. "Is that the reporter, thinks he's so smart?"

"He just sits...studying. That's what makes him so good." Muir finally responded.

"Boogey Man speaks, well what do you know."

Muir, not amused, glared at him for just a moment.

*****

Across the street, Blake sat in his little alcove watching the building, camera by his side. He was making notes in a small notebook, trying to kill time, hoping there would be some activity soon. He had spoken to Ed Doherty around six this morning. Doherty told him that there was an arrival of a freighter from Peru, due this morning. The ship's lading stated that it was loaded with sweatshop clothing and old machine parts.

After speaking with Doherty he contacted Morse, who confirmed, through dubious contacts, that the ship would be met off George's Island, just inside the harbor, and it's more valuable cargo unloaded, there. Morse could not confirm the identity of that cargo, but Blake figured that whatever it was was already inside the Bonner Warehouse.

What surprised him was the lack of activity. There were no cars out front and no one seemed to be guarding or, even watching the facility. He noted that the boat looked as though it had been moved, the mooring a good fifteen to twenty feet further back. He noted that yesterday he could see the entire wheelhouse from his perch, whereas, today, he couldn't even see the front windows. The bow was slightly askew, as well, seemingly lower in the water. Still, after what he observed of the frenzied activity in Florida, he was amazed by the stillness.

By ten thirty, he was getting edgy. He sensed that something was wrong, out of synch. He wanted to contact Morse, again, hoping to verify his information. Blake was not as patient as Muir had concluded and decided that he would walk back to his car and contact Morse for some confirmation of the transfer. However, he was curious and decided that before calling Morse he would take a closer look at that boat.

It had occurred to him that the cargoes might have been switched and that the drugs could have been dropped off at some other point along the harbor, East Boston, maybe, or Southie. He walked across the street, totally unaware that he was being watched from inside the building, reaching the parking lot and searching the grounds for some sign of life. Convinced that he was alone he made his way to the boat.

From the building behind Blake's, Pete watched what was happening and decided that Blake was taking too big a chance for him to follow too closely. For now, he would watch from across the street, convinced that he would be able to follow Blake's progress and still stay hidden from any prying eyes.

Blake got onto the boat, the decks slippery from the salt water that glided back and forth as the boat lightly bounced in the water. The lapping sound of seawater against the hull was all he could hear. He looked into the wheelhouse and found nothing of any interest, so he headed for the stern, where the hatch to the hold was located.

As he moved in that direction he noticed several sets of yellow rain gear strewn about the deck. He assumed the boat had been out and that the gear was left behind by deck hands in a great hurry to get off the boat. He wondered whether the crew had been spooked, possibly never making the switch, never taking anything off the freighter.

*****

Muir was standing by the back door, hastily pouring gasoline on the floor of the nearly empty building. Pierce was standing in the office doorway watching and wondering what he was up to. It had occurred to Pierce that even though Hoffman had no interest in Pierce's little moneymaking schemes, he had been a disruptive force that had already closed two entry ports to the smuggling conspirators. His other partners would not appreciate more interference.

Pierce's dilemma was a large one. None of his fellow smugglers knew anything about Muir. Any of them that might remember him, assumed, as did Pierce until last year, that he had long since perished at the hands of the Iranian Secret Police, having been arrested in Tehran in 1983 after a rare failed hit. Now was not a good time to reveal the identity of his traveling companion.

"What the hell do you think you're doing?!"

"Taking care of business." Hoffman put down the last can of gasoline and reached into his breast pocket for a gun. He glanced out the back window at the boat, then back at Pierce. Pierce was standing in what seemed a pool of his own sweat. He remembered just how uncontrollable Muir had always been.

"You're gonna whack the reporter, here? Why here?"

As he said that, Muir was fashioning a silencer to the end of his gun, then, when done, he stared into Pierce's eyes one last time. Pierce froze, knowing the look and the inevitable outcome. The first shot was enough to do the job, into the temple even though he was fifteen feet away from his prey. The second shot, delivered from above the lifeless body was pure pleasure.

He stood and admired his work. Now he was free to complete his task without the meddling of the oafish Pierce, a bad agent, a penny-ante blackmailer and a man with no stomach for the chase. He removed the silencer and started to put the gun back into his breast pocket when the back door opened and with sunlight behind, he saw the silhouetted figure of Blake standing there frozen at the sight of Pierce lying in a pool of blood, his face nearly gone.

Instinctually, he pulled the gun from its holster and fired at the reporter, hitting him near the stomach. Blake fell to his knees, clutching his torn midsection, staring up at Muir. He had never seen him before, had no idea who he was. Muir walked over to him and dragged him into the building, closed the door and lit the match that ignited the back of the building.

He knew Blake was still alive, but Blake had never been an intended victim, just a man who had bumbled into the wrong story at the wrong time. Once, the fire was started he opened the back door and threw a flaming board onto the boat deck, quickly engulfing the boat in flames, then headed for the far end of the dock to which he had tied a small motor boat.

He reached the boat and as he started down a short ladder he caught a glimpse of Pete scurrying around the corner making his way to the back door. Their eyes met for only an instant. He then disappeared and Pete was left with the astonishing feeling that he wasn't sure what he had just seen.

Pete had stayed across from the building, edging farther down the street so that he could see the boat behind the building. He watched as Blake entered the hold and then emerged, again, heading for the back door. The door opened and he caught the feint scent of gasoline, heard the gun's blast and saw the flash of light from the initial burst of flames.

As quickly as he could, he ran towards the building reaching the parking lot just as the boat became engulfed. Even though he feared an explosion once the fuel tanks were breached, he made his way to the back of the building in hopes of finding Blake alive. He paused just a moment as he reached for the door, catching the blur of a man running at the end of the pier.

Their eyes met and when he saw the smile on Muir's face he knew what he was going to find and that thought sent shivers down his spine and made his ankles week; a feeling he had only had once before, on a rainy night in the jungle over twenty-seven years ago in Vietnam.

He kicked the door open, something on the other side blocking his way. Once he had managed to push it open, he saw the entire inside of the building burning, the roof already giving way flames shooting up through the roof into the sky. When he looked down, he saw that it was Blake who was blocking his passage. He was alive and trying to hold himself together, coughing and hacking as the smoke filled his lungs.

Pete grabbed him under the arms and tried to turn him around, the dead weight making it nearly impossible. A loud crackle above alerted him to the loosening ceiling panels above him. He pulled Blake as hard as he could and was able to get him out of the way as the dangling metal sheets smashed not two feet from where he had found Blake.

The back entrance, blocked by burning metal fragments and plywood, was no longer an option for escape. He looked around, refusing to panic, locating the other door at the front of the building. He kneeled in front of Blake; "Just hang on for few more minutes and we'll be out of here."

He hoisted Blake over his shoulder and stumbled his way towards the door. More ceiling panels crashed as the entire rear of the building started to implode. Outside the flames had reached the fuel tanks and just as he reached the door he was knocked down by the tremendous force of the explosion. He was momentarily stunned, but pressed on, instincts pulling him towards safety. With one powerful kick he forced open the door and they were free of the deathtrap. He could no longer hold the weight over his shoulder. Placing Blake on the ground he dragged his semiconscious form to the edge of the parking lot as the first pieces of fire and rescue apparatus arrived.

Two large firemen descended upon them, taking Blake and rushing him to a waiting EMT. Pete glanced back at the water, searching, but never setting sight on the small boat with the smiling assassin. Through the heavy smoke and expanding flames he could barely see the water's edge, let alone any small craft. So engrossed was he, that he hadn't noticed the strips of cloth that hung from his shoulders where shirt sleeves had been or the burns along both forearms.

Blake had already been loaded onto an ambulance and two EMTs grabbed Pete, starting to work on his burns as Billy and Al came running into the parking lot. Seeing them, Pete collapsed to the ground, finally aware of what he had just done, of what he had just seen, of what had almost happened.

As the EMT cut away the last shards of material from his shoulders, he looked up and made eye contact with Billy. Pete formed a slight smile, eyes moistening slightly as Billy mouthed; "You done good."

The Emergency Room

Everett Memorial Hospital is an old, small community hospital that at the turn of the century was considered "state of the art" while, now, considered understaffed, underutilized and close to out of business. It was the kind of place that when you entered the front doors you would be immediately struck by the dark wood paneling, the hard stone floor and the four foot tall portraits, on every wall, of old men wearing bow ties, slicked down hair and elaborate, handlebar mustaches.

It was the closest hospital, on this side of the harbor to which an emergency could be directed. It didn't have a burn unit but it was capable of handling gunshot wounds, which, for Blake, was the primary concern. He was placed in an enclosed area away from the cubicles and examination rooms that composed the main patient area of the Emergency Room. A two man, armed detail stood outside the area as doctors came and went.

Pete, on the other hand, was seated on a gurney in one of the small curtained enclosures that lined the corridors. His wounds had been cleaned and dressed and he was waiting for a doctor, any doctor, to sign him out of there. By the time Billy and Alex arrived he was being cantankerous, yelling at nurses and refusing to answer any more questions being put to him by the Chelsea police.

Alex, upon seeing him, ran up and gave him a bear hug, while reminding him that he had promised to be careful. Billy stood back and laughed, then walked off towards the area where Blake was being treated. There was a policeman blocking his path to the end of the corridor, so he sat on a small bench and waited. He decided to let Alex have her moment with Pete, while he looked for someone who could update him on Blake's progress.

Soon a doctor emerged from Blake's enclosure and approached him. "Are you Billy?"

When he stated that he was, the doctor ushered him in to see Blake, telling Billy that Blake had asked to speak with him. Before they entered, he asked the doctor how it looked.

"I've seen worse recover…not many, but a few." He, then, turned and walked away.

Blake was awake, his eyes half open, his breathing labored. He was hooked up to a number of machines, recording devices and an IV. He raised an arm to motion Billy over to the bed. Billy complied, bending over and placing his ear close to Blake's mouth. In hoarse, halting tones Blake attempted to speak.

"My notes...Billy, you have to get my notes...got to keep them out of their hands..." Billy glanced around the room, locating Blake's clothes, figuring that the room key might be in one of the pockets. Blake was having trouble keeping his eyes open, so Billy decided to let him rest. He grabbed Blake's pants and took a card key out of the front pocket.

Then he walked back to the bed and placed a reassuring hand on Blake's shoulder. Blake opened an eye and gave a weak smile, then closed his eyes and went back to sleep. Billy looked at him once more, wondering if he would recover. He looked awful. His face was puffy, his arms and hands burned, his stomach wounded. Billy suddenly wished he had spoken to him about his years of resentment.

Out in the hall, Al and Captain Roselli were speaking to Pete. Remarkably neither Pete nor Roselli was screaming. Billy saw them all together and made his way to the group.

"What's up?"

Alex broke in; "Well, is he going to make it?"

"Too early to tell, Alex."

Everyone was silent for a brief moment. Roselli scratched his head and then turned to Pete.

"Did you see anyone there?"

"I told you, I saw Blake go into the building, a flash of light and then the boat burst into flames. I went into the building and dragged him out."

"I don't suppose you noticed the other body."

"What other body? When I got inside the place was pretty lit up. All I could think about was getting out of there and fast. I didn't see a second body."

This was, also, news to Billy. When he and Al left the scene, there had been no mention of a second body.

"Do they know who it was?" Billy believed that Blake was the target, but obviously, that might not have been the case. He reasoned that Blake had either been lured into the warehouse or had stumbled into something and had been shot to protect whatever nefarious activity was taking place. Now, it seemed as though he must have stumbled onto a murder.

Al told them that they couldn't identify the man as his face was practically shot off. The coroner was going to let them know when he had an ID, but not to expect something for several hours. In the meantime, the Chelsea PD was interested in getting some background on just what Blake was doing there. They told Roselli that Pete had been less than cooperative and that they expected he could get more information for them.

"I didn't tell them that I was aware of any investigation. But, isn't it odd how they reacted to your presence? Besides Billy and your friends, here, is there anyone who likes you?" Screamed the Captain.

Pete laughed for the first time since the incident. "Well, at least I know I haven't lost my touch."

"Take him home, will you. I'll think of something innocuous to tell my friends in Chelsea."

Billy had one piece of unfinished business. "Captain, can I borrow Al for a while. Blake asked me to go over to his place to grab his notes. He doesn't want them falling into the wrong hands."

"You okay with that?" Asked, Al.

"I trust you guys." Roselli nodded.

Alex interrupted; "Is there anyone we should be calling for him? What about family? Or, friends? Maybe a woman?"

"As far as I know, he doesn't have any family. The person I could think of would be his Producer."

"They've already contacted her. She's sending someone down from New York to take care of things." One of the doctors had volunteered that to Al. Alex shook her head and stared at Pete, putting a hand on his shoulder as he got his stuff.

The four friends left the hospital together, Alex taking Pete back to his place, while Al and Billy headed for the Hospitality Inn, where much of this affair had begun.

Ransacked

Al pulled into the parking lot, parking close to the main entrance. Billy had the key so they didn't have to stop at the front desk before heading upstairs. The lobby was quiet, a couple seated on a couch looking through the Boston dailies, a woman putting brochures in a rack by the Bell Captain's station, a man mulling around the entrance to the restaurant, nervously waiting for someone and a clerk busy behind the desk.

No one noticed them as they walked through the lobby, got on the elevators and disappeared to the upper floors of the hotel. They got off on Blake's floor, walking past the room where Muir had tried to break into Blake's room a couple of days earlier. The door to Blake's room was open, the door jam separated from the wall, the bolt popped free from it's casing.

Al drew his service revolver and went in first, insuring that the room was empty. Inside the room was a mess; drawers pulled free from the bureau, contents emptied onto the floor and bed, the mattress turned upside down, suitcases open and strewn about the room, pillow cases ripped and pictures pulled from the walls.

"God, how are we supposed to find anything in this mess?"

Al looked at Billy. "That's if there's anything left to find."

"Well let's hope we get lucky. I'll look around here, you try the bathroom."

Al took a pair of rubber gloves from his pocket and tossed them to Billy. "Be careful how you pick things up. At some point I'm going to have to call this in and I don't want the lab boys to be finding your prints all over the place."

Billy nodded, put on the gloves and started to ferret through the debris. Al went into the bathroom, which was similarly trashed. They pulled open suitcases, piles of clothes, shaving kits and books and papers by the nightstand.

They were getting discouraged when Al threw an empty gym bag at Billy. He caught the bag and looked questioningly at Al. "Feel kinda heavy?"

Billy weighed the bag in his hands. "I'll be a son of a bitch. You're right."

"Must be a false bottom." Billy reached inside and pulled along the edges of the bottom panel until one of them gave way. Inside was a small notebook and a roll of undeveloped film. Billy opened the notebook and laughed at seeing the notes encrypted. Al had walked beside him and didn't see the humor.

"How do you like that? This looks like the same encryption code I showed him years ago in Buffalo. I used to use it. In fact, I made it up. I had to show it to him so he could finish my story."

"What goes around comes around…Bill."

Al grabbed the film and stuffed it into his pocket, leaving Billy with the notes.

"You go decode those. I've got to call this in. I'll get these developed and let you know what I find."

"I'll be over at Pete's."

"Gotchya."

Billy took the notebook and made his way out the door and down to the lobby. The front desk was just receiving Al's call so no one noticed as he slipped out the front door and hailed a cab.

Chapter Nine

Revelations

The cab dropped Billy off at Pete's and the first thing Billy noticed was the presence of an Everett Police cruiser across from his driveway. Billy got out and waved to the officers, who had been there since Pete arrived from the hospital. It was late in the afternoon, so they were tired and hungry and waiting for the shift change that would occur at six.

Billy walked down the side of the house to the entrance to Pete's basement apartment and pulled out his key. He rang the bell as he unlocked the door, more to calm Alex than to announce his arrival. Upon entering he found Pete sitting on a stool in the kitchen area making toast while watching Alex fry some bacon.

The mayo, lettuce and tomato were sitting on the counter next to Alex. "When do we eat?"

Alex was embarrassed at the thought of having BLT's for supper, but she didn't want to leave Pete alone and that was all he had in the apartment that wasn't potato chips, ice cream or cereal. Billy could smell the freshly brewed coffee and suddenly remembered that he hadn't eaten all day.

Alex shooed Billy out of the kitchen so he sat on the couch and started to pour over Blake's notes. The notes were fairly extensive, outlining everything that Blake had told Billy. However, they were much more detailed. Blake went into great detail about the backgrounds of the two murdered men; detailing Hayes' activity as a CIA recruiter and how he served as the liaison to dozens of anti-Castro Cuban groups and their attempts to interfere with Castro's regime.

Blake tied Hayes to several men who trained Cuban nationals for the Bay of Pigs invasion and noted that he left service with the CIA shortly after being arrested for continuing to train guerrilla fighters after President Kennedy put a stop to the camps. Hayes spent no time in jail but appeared to retire from government life.

As for Cabrerra, he worked with Cuban exiles until the day he died, changing from a hard-core militant to a successful businessman in both Miami and New Orleans. Blake made note of several questionable contacts Cabrerra had within Organized Crime, as well as, with Hayes, who for years served as his contact with the US Government. In fact, many of his profitable business ventures were in shady businesses that most people associated with Organized Crime.

Blake tied both of these men to SG Enterprises which owned all of the businesses connected to the gun and drug smuggling operations. He had tried to follow some sort of a corporate ladder for this company but concluded that he had only identified the shadow company hiding the real owners of these businesses. It was in the description of the ownership web that the name of George Arliss surfaced for the first time in his notes.

As he continued to read, Arliss was mentioned three more times in reference to the operation. Curiously, Blake had asked around about this man and had yet to find anyone who knew who he was. Blake's notes pointed out that identifying him was becoming a focal point of the story. In fact, that was the primary reason he had hired Morse, thinking that if anyone in Boston knew him, an investigator with a lot of back room contacts would find him.

Most of what he read had already been explained to him. Other items he had learned on his own. In fact, he noted that he had a completely different angle than Blake and that, while he was going after an individual, Blake was pursuing an entire operation. Nothing in the notes gave Billy a clue as to the identity of the man he was following, in fact, nothing in the notes pertained to him, at all. The break-in was totally absent.

Eventually, the sandwiches were ready. Alex and Pete joined him on the couch, placing a plate and mug in front of him. Billy was too interested in getting through the notes to notice the food, right away. Alex and Pete just stared at him as if he were ignoring them. Finally, Billy looked up, surprised to see them sitting there.

"Interesting reading?" Pete was the first to comment.

"Pretty much. There's not much that we didn't already know."

"What about Bonner?"

"Just what we already know. He ties some of the strings together a little more neatly, but it's the same stuff. By the way, he's looking for a George Arliss as, sort of a, key figure in this whole thing. Says he may be the 'head of the snake', as he puts it."

Pete thought for a moment, trying to remember where he had heard the name before. He came up empty so he turned to his supper, wolfing down the sandwich and a handful of chips. Alex watched with some amusement, more satisfied that he was feeling okay, than amused by his unique table manners.

Billy sat upright as he reread a paragraph naming people he had identified with the smuggling scheme. "All of these people are either retired intelligence personnel or enforcers for the mob. If he's accurate, it's pretty evenly split."

"Also, sounds like they're pretty old." Pete's mouth was stuffed with chips. "By the way, I didn't say anything at the hospital, but I believe I saw our man leaving the scene. I'm not positive, but when I got to the back door, I looked down at the end of the pier and I could swear I saw him climbing down a ladder."

"You didn't think to mention that before now?" Alex was more than a little upset. She had been listening to Billy, but wasn't really paying attention. Now she was.

"I'm not sure that it was him. Besides, I didn't want to say anything to Roselli…just in case I was wrong."

"But, you weren't wrong, were you?" Alex was certain that Pete knew exactly what he saw.

"Really, Alex, I'm not sure."

"Well, there's nothing we can do about that now." Billy finished off his drink. "Whoever it was…I'm just glad you didn't confront him. Look what happened to Blake."

Alex walked back to the kitchen, got more coffee and some cookies and walked back to the couch, checking the dressing on Pete's arms before settling down. Billy continued to read through the notebook, stopping only to read a passage aloud or to have a bite or drink.

Blake made no references that Billy could match with the man who had shot him. In fact, he never seemed to be too concerned with who might have committed the murders, nor does he seem to believe that they are integral to the whole story. The notes were very detailed only in their descriptions of how the smuggling operation worked; where the drugs were entering the country and from where the weapons were stolen and how they were transported to the transfer points.

Blake did a lot of speculating about why either current or former government agents would be involved with such an endeavor, but none as to why two men with ties to the very group of people who were engineering the smuggling operation, were murdered either on or near the smuggling sites. The fact that both of these men were associated with clandestine anti-Castro operations that were eventually closed down by JFK was simply noted and then glossed over. That was most disappointing.

The Photo Lab

In the basement of the Everett Police Station was a small cramped photo lab. More a closet than a full-fledged dark room. It had been installed as an afterthought, when additional funding had been provided to upgrade the state of the city's forensic facilities. Unfortunately, space was at a premium so a closet designed for maintenance storage was modified for use as a dark room.

Al had called in the technician that ran the place and offered a dinner in exchange for some unauthorized overtime. While the technician was busy developing the film that they took from Blake's room, Al was back at his desk filing reports about the break-in and subsequent search of Blake's room. He kept Billy out of his report, even though the Captain knew he was there.

It was close to seven by the time the technician called him to say his prints were ready. Al finished his report as quickly as he could, then headed for the basement. The technician had laid out the drying prints on a long white table opposite the dark room. When Al arrived he stood at the table searching for anything that might shed some light on what had happened. Not knowing when the pictures were taken was an obvious problem, but he was, at least hoping to recognize someone.

There were over twenty pictures, mostly of men coming and going at the Bonner warehouse. A couple of men looked like low-level hoods, recognized for past run-ins with the department. He figured that they could be easily picked up whether the Everett Police had jurisdiction or not. Halfway across the table he spotted a picture of Pierce entering the building with an older man who had an arm draped across Pierce's shoulder.

He wasn't sure how important that was, aside from tying all the stories together. He speculated that if Pierce were driving the "hit and run" car, then he would not have wanted to attract attention. However, if he was covering for someone, then it had to be someone who was even more important to the operation.

As he was studying the rest of the pictures, Roselli came walking in.

"What have you got, there, Al?"

"I'm not sure. A couple of Revere hoods and that guy Pierce are the only people I can ID from this lot."

"Pierce? Are you sure? Let me see that?" Roselli was animated. Though, not exactly a stoic, brooding man the captain was usually composed and thoughtful. Years ago, while still in the military, he found that allowing his emotions to impact his performance or demeanor was counterproductive. That was why Al was so stunned by the outburst.

Al handed the picture to Roselli, who stared at it intently. The two men pictured outside the

Bonner warehouse were Pierce and Arthur Cogent. The captain became ridged and his face flushed with anger.

“What’s up Cap? What’s wrong?”

“For starters, I just got a call from the Coroner’s Office. That other body was Pierce.”

“You’re not serious?”

“Shot in the face at close range.”

“Our boy?”

“I’d say that’s a pretty good bet or he’d be the one in the morgue.”

Roselli stared at the picture, wondering just what Cogent’s connection to the smuggling operation was. After the last couple of days he was convinced that Cogent was not as retired as he said he was. Now, it was time to flush him out.

“You said ‘for starters’, what else?”

“This other guy? I know him. He’s retired CIA…or so he says. I’m going to hold on to this picture. It’s time I paid Arthur a call.”

Roselli stormed out. Al gathered all the remaining pictures and headed for Pete’s.

Serino's Storage

By the time Al got to Pete's apartment the three friends were trying to decide whether or not Blake's notes were complete or if they had somehow missed another set of notes. Billy assumed that some of the background material might be on Blake's home or office PC and that the notes they found were only what he needed to have with him.

It was Pete's contention that they were giving Blake too much credit. He thought that the notes seemed pretty thorough for a show like America's Front Page. After all, he argued, they had never let facts get in the way of ruining someone's life in the past. So, he continued, it followed that all Blake was looking for was the hint of impropriety so that he could squeeze a couple of Washington bureaucrats into retirement.

Billy and Alex thought that a little too simplistic, though not beyond the realm of possibility. Al rang the bell and interrupted the flow of the argument. Alex let him in. By the time he had reached the couch he had told them of the pictures and that the second man in the fire was Pierce. There was a short quiet moment to process the new information, before Alex, then Billy sounded their concerns.

"If that was Pierce, then our man is on his own, free of his shadow."

"...and free to do whatever he might want to do...hurt who he needs to hurt."

Alex pointed to Pete. "He must've seen you if you saw him."

"You saw this guy at the scene of the fire and you didn't tell anyone?" Al was furious.

"I said I thought I saw him, I'm really not certain...though I think we can assume..."

The sentence drifted into dead space as they all considered what had to be done next.

"I'd love to see what is inside that storage bin." Billy had been curious about what might be stored there since he visited Pierce's near-empty house.

"I don't think Roselli will appreciate that."

"Is that important?" Pete agreed that it was the next logical move, though without Al's help there would be a lot of trouble if they got caught.

Al knew he was fighting a losing battle. "Look, the Captain is out looking for the other guy in the picture with Pierce. He says he's a retired CIA something or other. He knows him, but I'm not certain from where."

"That should buy us some time, Al. What do you say...can you get us in."?

"I'm glad my pension is vested."

Alex tried to stop them, but it was too late. She thought that Billy would back off but he was certain that they would find something that would help clarify what was going on. Al asked her to stay at Pete's until they returned, just in case Roselli tried to get a hold of him. Reluctantly, she agreed.

Once outside, Al dismissed the police detail, explaining that he would be with them for rest of the evening and that they needn't return until midnight. Once that was done they piled into Al's car and drove towards the Parkway. As with everything in Everett, it was a short ride, a quarter mile or so down Broadway on to Ferry Street to an intersection with the Parkway, half a block from Serino's Secure Storage facilities.

One of the daytime uniforms was on duty as the security officer at the main gate. The storage facility was a large complex consisting of one large brick building with five or six floors of various sized storage pens and several two-story metal framed cargo containers ringing a large open yard where rental trucks from the U-Rent, next door, were parked for the night. The facility allowed for twenty-four hour access, but there was no one about when Al walked into the security shack at the front gate.

It took only a few minutes for Al to explain the situation and get the location to Pierce's locker, on the third floor of the old brick building. The gates were opened and Billy and Pete drove to the side of the shack where Al gave them the directions and the bad news that each renter was responsible for obtaining their own security devices. Now inside the facility they drove over to the front of the building, parked Al's car and, carrying the metal cutters Al gave them, they entered the building and climbed the stairs to the third floor.

It took a couple of minutes to get their bearings, but they quickly found the row of storage bins where C232 was located. This was an area of large bins, roughly eight feet long, ten feet high and eight feet deep. There were four to each corridor, Pierce's being tucked against an inside wall. Each bin had a six-foot high metal door with six-foot walls topped by four feet of chicken wire. The locker next to Pierce's was empty. Since there was no lock on the door, Pete fired up the lantern they had brought and checked out the inside of the container.

The four foot high chicken wire partition went all the way around the top of each space. They decided that they would enter from the empty bin so as to conceal their cutting. Billy gave Pete a boost and he started to cut into the wire frame, one link at time. The wire was close to being a mesh, so it took a long time to make a hole large enough for the two men to crawl through.

Once done, Pete lowered himself down into Pierce's bin, turned on the lantern and signaled Billy to follow. Billy could hear some noise from the bin as Pete moved a large couch to a position right under the opening. He stood on it's back and leaned his head through the opening. Billy jumped up and caught hold of the lower edge of the hole and Pete grabbed his shirtsleeve. It took a couple of minutes but Billy made his way through the hole and into the bin.

In the subdued light given off by the lantern it should have been difficult to see what was stored, here, but as they surveyed the room they noticed only two items. The first was the enormous couch; three cushions wide with large high armrests. That was against one wall. On the opposite side there were several boxes, two of which were open. Other than that, the space was empty.

Pete pulled the cushions from the couch and by moving the lantern closer could make out the seams of a hidden compartment in the base of the chair. He pulled the fabric away and the two of them found themselves staring at an arsenal of weaponry. There were four scoped rifles, several handguns, a couple of automatic weapons and ammunition for each one.

“Now, we know why this wasn’t in the Living room over at Pierce’s place.”

Pete looked over his shoulder at Billy and laughed. “You imagine what kind of damage this guy could do with an arsenal like this? Now, the question is whether or not these guns belong to Pierce or our guy.”

“Nothing in Pierce’s background would suggest these are his. This looks like a hit man’s collection.”

Pete picked up a couple of the smaller guns and looked them over. Then he reached down and opened a box of ammunition.

“Hollow points. Nasty stuff.”

Billy had taken a few sheets of paper and made some notes regarding what was in the couch, then grabbed the lantern and turned towards the boxes against the opposite wall.

“Come on, let’s check these out.”

They crossed the room and started to pull the boxes apart. One box was filled with nothing but newspaper clippings, mostly faded yellow, one or two a bit more current. Billy picked up one that looked familiar. It was the New Orleans paper with the article about Cabrerra's death. Underneath was a Miami Herald with a small article about Hayes' death.

Billy looked at Pete; "Looks like this guy likes to keep his press clippings."

Meanwhile, Pete was foraging through a second box and found more of the same; newspaper articles about various unsolved murders, some from as far away as Australia.

"This guy gets around..." Pete said as he showed an international paper to Billy. "...after all, you know how hard it is to get good help these days."

Billy moved the top box and peered into the one under it. Inside that box he found a series of manila folders, with names and addresses in each one. Most of the addresses were either in Washington DC or a neighboring community. Inside each folder were newspaper articles, lists of what seemed to be various government operations, pictures of individuals and copies of wires and in some cases Faxes, all from Pierce to the names on the outside of the envelopes.

"Pete, what do you make of these?"

Pete put down the newspaper articles he had been perusing and looked at a couple of the folders that Billy had in his hands.

"Blackmail?" Billy asked.

"Could be. Hey, didn't Fox say that his friend in DC said Pierce was a major screw up?"

"That's right."

"Well, I bet, now we know how he kept his job."

Billy counted sixteen file folders. "He's a collector of information. I wonder if he has a file on our friend?"

They each took a bunch of folders, searching for names that they might recognize. They looked at the pictures in each, for a possible match to the man whose identity they sought. There were no matches, but Billy found a folder with the name George Arliss penciled on the outside tab. Inside, Billy found several articles dating back to the late fifties, outlining various unsolved murders in Havana, Peru and Costa Rica.

This folder, much thicker than the others, also contained several pictures one of which Billy recognized. It was the famous "Tramps" picture he had seen a few nights before in the JFK Library.

"Pete, you've got to see this. Bring the lantern closer."

Pete moved the lantern directly above the picture. The picture was faded a bit but you could still make out the images fairly clearly. Circled in red ink were three of the four men. They both stared at the first, most clearly visible figure.

"I don't know about you, Scoop, but that looks just like our man. Look, add a little gray hair and a few wrinkles..."

Billy noticed the same thing. "Oh my God! Let's get out of here. I want to talk to Fox."

Pete agreed, but as he was putting the news clippings back into one of the boxes he noticed a large stuffed manila envelope lying on the bottom of the carton. He pulled it out and opened it up. Inside was a partial manuscript: "My Life in the Shadows" by George Arliss.

He showed it to Billy; "What do you make of this?"

"That's the book Roselli is looking for...but I don't think that's the right author. Roselli was looking for an Arthur Cogent."

"Maybe there's some reference to him in one of these folders."

They looked through the entire stack of folders, but found no mention of Arthur Cogent.

"Let's take some of this stuff and get out of here."

Pete agreed. "You don't have to ask me twice."

Confrontation

Captain Roselli sat in his car, just a few steps from the front entrance to the Revere Dog Track, trying to decide if he should confront Cogent on his own turf. He was staring at two pictures. One was the picture of Cogent and Pierce at the warehouse and the other was of the perp whose identity, he was certain, Cogent would know.

After several minutes he decided he was wasting time and that it wouldn't really matter. Arthur was a man who was always in control, so it would make no difference where he approached him.

He got out of his car, entered the track and walked to the clubhouse. Their usual table was deserted, unusual for this early in the program, so he scouted the room for a familiar face. By the pari-mutuel windows, he spotted Gil Holland chomping on a cigar counting his winnings, the cigar bouncing as if he was trying to count out loud. He couldn't see Cogent or Harry Blair, for that matter.

He lay back by the table and watched for any sign of the other two men. Holland was off buying something to eat so, at the moment, he was alone. After a couple of minutes he spotted Harry Blair walking back from the Men's room.

Roselli saw him and the two exchanged pleasantries before sitting down. Harry noticed that the captain was preoccupied and didn't press him for an explanation, but judging by the past couple of evenings they had spent together he surmised that he was looking for Cogent.

"Arthur's downstairs talking to an old friend of his. He should be back, soon."

"It's that obvious?"

"I've known you a long time and I don't think I've ever seen anyone get under your skin the way Arthur has."

"He's such an arrogant SOB." Roselli scanned the room.

"He sure can be a pain in the ass, but that's just his way."

"I'm sorry, Harry, but I don't buy that. He really thinks he's superior. It's like he's the only one who knows what's going on. Always acts like he's on to some great secret that the rest of us 'mortals' just wouldn't understand."

"You may be right. He was at the agency for over forty years. I'll bet he does know some things that we wouldn't want to know. For that matter, all of us have seen our share of hidden truths. Its all part of being in this business...you know that"

"That's just it, he acts like he's still in the business."

They sat there, quietly, for a couple of minutes, both men looking around, trying to ignore the mounting tension. Roselli was getting restless. Again, wasting too much time waiting to confront this man. Harry spotted Gil slowly ambling his way back to the table holding a plate of cheese fries and sipping a beer. When he reached them the silence was broken by an exchange of pleasantries.

Gil placed the fries on the table and told them to dig in. Harry grabbed a couple, then stopped when he saw Arthur at the top of the stairs, walking with a man whose identity was unknown to him. The two paused after reaching the top step where they shook hands and parted company. Cogent walked straight to the betting windows, scanning his program as he walked.

Roselli watched intently. Cogent had his tickets, then turned towards his friends and immediately made eye contact with Roselli. There was a glint in his eye, he could see the cold expression on Roselli's face.

"Boys. How's the investing tonight?" Cogent asked as he reached the table.

"Not bad, Arthur." Gil smiled through a mouth full of food.

"And you, Captain?"

"I didn't come here to gamble, tonight."

Cogent sat down. "I didn't think so. What's on your mind?"

Roselli placed the picture of Arthur and Pierce in front of him. He examined it and a slight smile crossed his face.

"And this is?"

"The other man in that picture is dead. Shot and left to burn in an arson job in that building." He pointed to the Bonner warehouse.

"I hadn't heard."

"What's going on, here?"

"You obviously have drawn your own conclusions."

They stared at each other, ignoring their two companions. Roselli placed the second picture in front of Cogent. He didn't look at it right away, then glanced down at it. It took a couple of seconds to register, then his expression changed and the blood drained from his face.

He stared at the police photo of Hoffman Muir.

"Who is he, Arthur?"

"Where'd you get this picture?"

"This is the guy you were going to help me identify."

"I can't help you."

He stood up and turned to walk away.

"That's it!? You know who this guy is. Tell me!"

He turned back to him. "That man is dead." Then he walked away. Roselli stood up, but Gil stopped him from pursuing Cogent. They all watched him disappear down the stairs.

Gil broke the silence. “What was that all about? I’ve never seen him rattled before. Never.”

Chapter Ten

George Arliss

Al dropped Billy off at the newspaper where Fox and Claire were waiting for him. In the meantime he and Pete would pick up Alex and meet them there to go over everything they had taken from the locker. Though Al was not entirely comfortable with the idea of taking items from the storage facility, he realized that short of arresting his two friends he would be unable to prevent it.

Billy entered the office with a box of clippings and the manuscript that they had found. He gave the manuscript to Fox who immediately recognized it as the book Roselli was after. Just as Billy had been, Fox was surprised at the name of the author. The difference was that he recognized George Arliss.

"Billy, do you know what you have, here?"

"I assumed it was the book Roselli was so hot for."

"Oh, it's that all right...but haven't you ever heard the name George Arliss before?"

"Not that I recall, no."

Claire came over and sat next to Fox at one of the terminals. She started to type something into the system. Quickly she was on the Net searching for some information.

"Who is he?"

Fox looked over at what Claire was doing, waited a second or two and then pointed to the screen. Billy walked behind her and read the title of a web site.

"House Select Committee on Assassinations. You know Arliss from there?"

"He's one of those behind the scenes guys with power that no one ever hears about. We did a huge series of articles on the committee and he was a very prominent figure in their investigation. I know he had something to do with the early efforts to overthrow Castro, but I'm not sure what else. It's been what, 20 years since that committee finished its work."

"Something like that." Claire agreed. "I seem to remember him at the hearings, so smug and arrogant. Nothing could touch him. There was a whole group of CIA types, just like him. All acted the same way. It disgusted me."

Billy was reading the screen. Arliss was an employee of the CIA, thought to be alive, but whereabouts unknown. He worked as a member of the OAS, a high-ranking CIA official with contacts to the Chilean military, before the Allende assassination, was in charge of CIA efforts in both Guatemala and the Dominican Republic and headed the CIA operation to oversee the training of Cuban ex-patriots by US based mercenaries in Florida and Louisiana in the early sixties.

He was the suspected contact between organized crime and the CIA during the time when they were both trying to find a way to assassinate Castro. Again, a program terminated by Kennedy.

Following the Bay of Pigs, he was one of the targets of the JFK-led CIA purges. While he served no jail time, he was demoted after JFK had the military camps closed. His friendship with Allen Dulles, the deposed head of the CIA, was also mentioned in the write-up.

Billy sat down and let out a huge sigh. “If this is the guy who wrote ‘A Life in the Shadows’, then who the hell is Arthur Cogent?”

“Let’s go through some of this stuff you brought before we draw any conclusions. Don’t go off the deep end.” Fox had gotten up and walked over to the box of files and news clippings. He pulled out the files and read off the names.

"Hurly, Wintrop, Glassen, Reed...all top men at either the CIA or Justice. Did you look at what is in these folders?"

"Looks like blackmail. Pierce must have gathered something on every one of those guys. How else could a buffoon like him keep his job?"

Claire turned around from the computer screen. "It didn't protect his life, though, did it?"

"No, but you can bet one of these people didn't have him hit, or they would already have possession of these files." Fox continued to thumb through the files.

"What if the one person that had him hit only took one folder...his? He might not care if the rest of these people got embarrassed." Billy was leafing through the manuscript as he spoke.

"You could be right about that."

The phone rang. Claire picked it up, listened for a moment and then turned to Fox and Billy. "Alex wants to know if they should pick up something to eat."

"I'm too excited to eat." Billy put down the manuscript and grabbed one of the printouts Claire had generated from the Net, trying to match it to the information in the folders, so far to no avail.

Claire told them to come straight over and forget the food, no doubt disappointing Pete. She put the phone down and went back to scanning for more information about Arliss and the House Committee on Assassinations. She tried to scan each article she pulled, almost impossible because there was so much information on the site.

At last she hit upon something useful; Arliss was Pierce's direct supervisor when he was assigned to the embassy in Mexico City. This information, coupled with the picture of the two of them outside Bonner, hinted at a long term relationship, leaving the three of them to conclude that either Pierce had something big on Arliss or Pierce and Arliss were working together.

Meanwhile, Fox was focusing on the George Arliss folder. He was reading a government document stamped 'Top Secret' that alluded to a sabotaged Cubana Airlines plane that was blown out of the sky in 1976. The document declared that the arrest of two low level Venezuelan nationals would be sufficient for the Barbados authorities and that there would be no need for additional disinformation. Someone had penciled in Arliss' name as the author of the memo.

"You know some of this stuff rings a bell, but nothing really specific. I wonder if there is anything in that manuscript that will confirm any of this."

Billy was now pouring through the newspaper clippings. "Probably with some twisted slant." Finally, he found what he was looking for…the 'Tramps' photo. He got up and walked over to Fox and showed it to him. "What do you make of this?"

Fox held the picture, a look of shock and anger. "Oh my God! Claire come here. You've got to see this."

Claire got up and rushed over to Fox. "I don't believe it." She walked over to the front counter and grabbed a copy of their paper. Putting the front page side by side with the 'Tramps' photo they both could see the resemblance. "What do you think?"

"I don't even want to speculate." Fox was dumbfounded.

"Before you do, you should know that Pete thinks he saw that guy at Bonner. He figures he killed Pierce and that Blake must have stumbled into it."

"That's just great! This guy has been running around Everett and following you." Claire started to pace. "Where is Al?"

Billy walked over to Fox. "Could he be the man?"

"You mean the real JFK shooter? Grassy Knoll and all that?"

"Yeh."

"Billy, I just don't know for sure. Do you know how many good people have been looking for that guy? Must be hundreds, if not thousands."

"You agree this guy's some sort of pro."

"No doubt. He's a hit man and I'd say by all the trappings, he works both sides of the fence. I don't doubt that for a minute, but I don't think he's an actual agent."

"We've got a hit man, arrested within minutes of the Kennedy assassination and you're reluctant to say he shot the man?"

Claire was getting more agitated, walking back and forth to the windows and then back to Fox and Billy. "Stop it, both of you! I want you to call Roselli if Al doesn't get here in the next few minutes."

"Calm down. We're safe, here."

As Fox said that there was a crash in the back of the building, then the lights went out. Claire screamed, Fox put his arms around her and pulled her to the floor. The back door opened and, in silhouette they could see the figure of Hoffman Muir. He entered the room slowly, a handgun glistening in the streams of light that shown through the large windows. It was dark but not black. The streetlights gave the room an eerie illumination that made everything look gray.

He stepped to middle of the room. "No one has to get hurt. I want his address. I don't care about the rest of it."

Billy was crouched behind the front counter, but stood and spoke to Muir. "Whose address?"

"You're the hotshot reporter, you tell me." Muir turned on a flashlight and pointed his gun at Billy. "You have two minutes. Where do I find, Arliss?"

A sudden flash of red and blue lights appeared in front of the building, both Billy and Muir turning towards the street. Fox and Claire made a run for the door, Billy dove out of the way and Muir fired a shot in his direction. The shot missed its mark and Billy fell to the floor as Al entered the room. He reached for the light switch and the front of the room became illuminated. Muir was gone.

Pete and Alex were close behind and ran to Fox and Claire huddled together close to the doorway. Al moved cautiously to the back of the building, Billy close behind. He found no one there, the back door open and no sign of anyone running away from the scene. He examined the door. It had been jimmied.

"It's a good thing we didn't stop for dinner. What was he after?"

"All he wanted was an address."

"An address? Whose?"

"George Arliss. The author of the book that Roselli wanted…though that wasn't the name he gave us."

"Well, let's get a hold of him and bring him up to date. He might know who this guy is."

Connections

Roselli sat at the clubhouse table with Harry and Gil wondering what his next move would be. Harry had asked who the men in the two pictures were, but the captain didn't answer. They sat there for an eternity, without speaking. Eventually, Gil got up, walked to the betting windows and resumed his evening's pursuit. After getting his betting slips he walked downstairs and out towards the finish line to watch the race.

Harry tried to get Roselli to talk but he was too upset. He and Roselli had served together during Vietnam and for a short term after they had been sent home. He had never seen the captain so preoccupied, so lost in thought. It was as if he were watching a volcano getting ready to erupt. The veins on the side of Roselli's head were bulging as he stared off, lost in thought.

The silence was broken as Roselli's pocket beeper went off. He grabbed the device and noted the number. Then, without saying a word, he got up and walked to the nearest security office, asked to use the phone and called Al at the Everett Post Gazette. Al informed him of what had just transpired at the paper. This infuriated the captain and he told Al to stay with Billy and wait for his call.

After slamming down the phone, he took off in the direction of Gil Holland. Finding Cogent's close friend outside, along the rail by the finish line. Gil saw him coming and considered fleeing, but also reasoned that out in the open Roselli would be more reasonable. He was still smart enough to be a little scared.

Roselli approached him head on. "Gil! I want to know where that bastard is, now!"

Gil didn't say anything, looking around making certain that there were enough people around to protect him if Roselli became unreasonable.

Face to face, the captain glared into his eyes and repeated himself. "Gil, tell me where the hell he is."

"I don't think that's a very good idea, Cap. You don't know who you're messing with. No one has ever come out on top after going up against him."

"I don't like being played for a fool. I'm going to ask you one more time. Where is he? This time it's his life I'm worried about. That animal is after him and I want to know where he is, now!!"

"Let him worry about that animal. He's not in any danger, trust me."

"Just tell me where he lives, 'cause if this guy gets to him first he won't be able to stop him."

Gil looked down and then reached into his pocket for a pen. He wrote Cogent's address down on a corner of his program and handed it to Roselli. "If what you say is true, fine. But if it isn't, you're gonna have to deal with both of us."

Silence

Pete was lying on his couch, arm shielding his eyes as Billy paced the area in front of the kitchen counter. Alex was busying herself by trying to concentrate on correcting a stack of papers she took home from school. Al was seated watching the evening news on one of the local stations, half listening to stories dealing with hazardous waste cleanups, stalled legislation and the failures of the local sports teams. No one was talking. They were waiting for Roselli to call back.

Frustrated by the silence, Alex walked into the kitchen, opened the fridge and grabbed a bottle of soda, slamming the door as she put the beverage on the counter. The noise startled Pete who glanced over his shoulder in her direction. Billy walked up behind her and massaged her shoulders. She smiled and nuzzled his hand as it sat on her shoulder.

"Sorry 'bout that. This waiting is awful." She said softly.

"I know it's not what we want to be doing right now."

"What is it that you'd like to do? I'm probably more afraid of that than anything else."

"We just want to catch the guy, that's all."

She looked away from him, opening one of the cabinets and grabbing a glass.

"This guy is a trained killer. You guys are amateurs, even Al and the police. I don't trust you not to get hurt. I'm sorry, but I'm scared."

She shook his hand off her shoulder, picked up her drink and went back to the table and sat down, staring blankly at the pile of unread papers.

Finally, the phone rang and Al quickly answered it.

"Captain? Right...no we're all just a bit on edge... But, we don't have any jurisdiction, there. Okay, I'll tell everyone to sit tight...By the way, we have a copy of that manuscript you were looking for...Yeh, but it's by a George Arliss...Let me take care of some things, here, and then I'll run it over to you...Alright."

After he hung up he told the rest what Roselli had said. "He's outside Cogent's house in Revere. There's no one there, so he's going to sit on it for a while. He can't confirm that this guy is Arliss, but he believes he is and he has pretty good instincts."

"What are we supposed to do in the meantime?" Billy wanted to know.

"He says to sit tight and tomorrow morning we'll figure out how we're going to trap this guy. A good night's sleep is probably the best idea."

Pete was already drifting off on the couch. Billy asked Al if he was going to stay with them, there, or head home. "I'm going to run home and get some sleep. I'll get a detail to your place so you can go home too. Oh, let me have that manuscript, Captain wants me to run it over to him before I go home."

Billy asked Alex her plans and she said she would stay with Pete. Billy decided to stay with them, as well. Al made a call to the station and reassured his friends that there would be a car outside all night. After grabbing the manuscript, he looked out the window and waited for his relief.

*****

In Revere, Roselli sat in his car staring at the large Tudor home that sat across the street directly on the beach at the end of a long side street. There were several large houses along this stretch of beach. This section of Revere is called Point of Pines where a large amount of well-to-do individuals lived directly on the water's edge.

The shoreline was a perfect crescent curve, the public beach dominating most of its distance. From the location of Cogent's house you could look across the bay at the island of Nahant, in one direction and to the peninsula of Winthrop in the other. None of that mattered to Roselli as he decided to take a look at the ocean side of the property.

He got out of his car, crossed the street, walked to the edge of the property and down a path to the seawall. He surveyed the beach as far he could see. He noted that not a soul stirred. He walked up to the deck at the rear of the house and looked through the glass sliders. There were no lights, no movement and no sounds coming from inside.

He turned and went back to his car, to spend the rest of the night.

*****

It was approaching midnight as Fox and Claire sat across from each other at their kitchen table. They had been unable to sleep, Fox not even trying to lie down. Claire had gone to bed but without Fox she didn't give it a serious try. So they sat at the table, Fox drinking a glass of milk, Claire a cup of tea.

"I'll never be able to say it enough, but thanks for thinking of me tonight." Claire reached across the table and patted Fox's hand.

"I couldn't imagine anything happening to you. It wouldn't be worth getting up in the morning." His eyes moistening as he said it.

"Well, let's not worry about that for a few more years, yet, anyway. Come on, let's go sit on the couch." She got up and took Fox by the hand and the two of them walked into the living room and sat on the couch. Claire nestled her head onto Fox's shoulder as he put his arm around her.

*****

Pete was sound asleep on the couch, never having moved since the time Al left. Alex sat in a chair, her legs curled up under her staring at Pete as he slept. She had a pillow in back of her and a blanket across her lap but she didn't feel much like sleeping.

The events of the day kept going through her mind; Blake getting shot, the fire, Pete's heroism, the realization that they were chasing a professional killer and then the killer showing up at the Gazette. The longer she thought on these events the more she tried to figure out what had happened to shake the tranquility of their once quiet lives.

Billy was standing in the kitchen staring at Alex, admiring the way she looked at Pete and wishing he had followed Al's advice and gone home to his own apartment so she and Pete could be alone. He was too shaken to sleep, himself, so he was spending his time re-reading Blake's notes, sifting through the files and putting a more concise spin on the facts. He had tried to write a story for tomorrow's edition but he had waited too long to make the printer's deadline.

From his research, he could see a pattern to Pierce's blackmail. He had spent years gathering information on some of the most respected members of the Intelligence community, often using their own tools against them. Apparently he was a great listener who made copious notes and then gathered little bits of information to back up his notes.

Most of the men were not in his direct chain of command, so he wouldn't have to use the gathered information unless they came at him. The records didn't reveal when or how he had used the information, just that he had. Some of the notes indicated sums of money changing hands, others hinted at favors done.

Beside the blackmail information, he worked through the scrapbook of newspaper clippings. All of the articles contained information about various deaths. Most of the deceased were prominent men, some apparently having 'staged' accidents, others outright hits.

As for information concerning the JFK assassination, there was the 'Tramps' photo, an article about Pierce, himself, regarding the erroneous identification of Oswald in Mexico City and another article regarding the last minute change in the route of the presidential motorcade.

Billy made his notes and kept coming to the same conclusion; they had stumbled onto two separate criminal enterprises. He wrote his story, telling of the drugs for guns operation and then detailing how that was being destroyed by a hired gun with his own agenda. He didn't bother to describe the killer as the man who may have fired the deadly shot at JFK. This was Kennedy country and before you raise the specter of his death you had better be a lot more confident than he was about who they had in their sights.

Billy had watched Alex for several minutes and her eyes never left the sleeping Pete. He looked so peaceful, it was as if he knew he had an angel watching over him. Billy was glad one of them would be sharp and alert in the morning. He grabbed a glass of water and then went back into Pete's bedroom intending to continue his research.

*****

Outside Pete's apartment, Al sat in an unmarked car. He was drinking coffee from a thermos and listening to his police radio. A car had been stationed out in front of Pierce's place and he was getting regular updates from the officers there.

When he left Pete's, he did go home for a short while. He was restless, like a caged animal. When he realized that sleep would be impossible he sat alone in the dark, in his family room and watched the late news. After two or three stories, he had seen enough. He knew it was his responsibility to protect his friends so he called the station and told them that he was going back on duty, outside Pete's.

Being on the scene made him feel better even if it did not ease the tension or help him devise a means to catch their predatory madman.

*****

Roselli was back in his car watching for Cogent to come home. He had been there for nearly six hours and there was no sign of him. Now, he too sat in the dark, trying to read the manuscript by streetlight and listening for footsteps in the dark.

*****

A squad car sat in front of Pierce's rented house on Baldwin Ave. The two officers were aware of the importance that both Roselli and Al had placed on their assignment. They respected both men to such a high degree that they were determined to stay focused and alert until their shift was over at six.

Inside the house in the third floor attic, Hoffman Muir sat in the dark, staring down at the street through the slats in the eaves of the house, watching the squad car. He had already gotten a couple of hours of sleep on the little boat, which he tied up at an abandoned pier in East Boston, a dead homeless man attested to his resolve to end this final mission in the morning.

Muir sat silently until it was nearly dawn. Just as the first traces of light were appearing above the horizon he quietly got up and made his way downstairs. The two officers were awake and watching the front of the house. Muir stopped in the back hall and grabbed a gas canister, then, slipped out the back door, walked to a secluded spot behind the garage and disappeared through a hole in the fence.

Chapter Eleven

The Head of the Snake

April 19th: Patriot's Day

Roselli sat in his car as the sky began to lighten. Beyond the rows of homes he could see the sun reflecting on the facades of the glass and stone condominiums along the beach. He had looked through as much of the book as he could in the diminished light and had found a large gap in the chronology it was attempting to portray. There were mentions of contact and assistance to Castro, even a personal contact with him in 1958, but nothing from the point of his ascension to power until a chapter referencing the Nixon years.

While it was interesting reading, he found nothing that was helpful in identifying his quarry or in gaining a true insight into Arthur Cogent or George Arliss. He glanced at his watch, noting the time as five thirty.

At the far end of the street a single car turned onto the road, lights off, slowly moving towards Roselli's position. He couldn't make out the driver, so he watched the car as it approached and passed him, all the while slowing almost to stop. It turned into Cogent's driveway and stopped. The door flung open and a tired, hunched over Arthur Cogent got out. As he headed for the front door, the Captain took advantage of the slow pace of his walk and caught up to him.

He surprised him, but there was no confrontation. Cogent simply looked at him and smiled. "What took you so long?"

"I've been here all night."

"Let's get inside. We need to talk."

Cogent unlocked the front door, turned off his alarm and the two men entered his home. It was spacious, open. Inside the front entranceway was a set of steps that led down to a large expansive living room with a couple of leather couches, a large screen television, a full service bar and sliding glass doors to the back yard.

Cogent walked straight to the bar and poured himself a scotch. He offered the bottle to Roselli and he showed two fingers as Arthur poured a small amount of the liquid into a snifter. He grabbed the two glasses and pointed to the couches, he on one, the Captain on the other.

"What's on your mind?" He handed a snifter to Roselli.

"You look like you've been through hell."

"Never mind that. Why are you here?"

"You know damn well? Who is he?"

"You don't want to know. Just drop it. He'll be on his way pretty soon and you'll never hear from him, again."

"You know that for a fact? So far he's attempted to kill, at least two people and succeeded in killing a third."

"Trust me, if he wanted to kill all three of them, he would have. He's the best."

Roselli took a deep swig from his glass. "I don't get it. Why is this guy, here? What's he after? You seem to know more than you ever let on."

"I know you don't believe me, but until you showed me that picture, I was certain that vermin was dead. Up until then, I just thought you had some minor league, third rate hood."

"Obviously, he's much more than that?"

"He's simply the most efficient killing machine our lack of faith ever created."

"You still haven't told me who he is…or, for that matter where you've been and why you look like this."

Cogent got up from his seat and walked over to the sliding glass doors, pulling the sheer curtains aside and staring off at the brightening sky. "Tonight, I've been to almost every man who owes me something and not one of them would have anything to do with me, despite what I know about them and what I could tell the world. That is the power of this man."

"Why do you need their help?"

Cogent spun around and fired back. "Don't you get it? It's me he's here to kill!"

"Are you sure?"

"Oh, please, Roselli! Now you sound like some naive schoolboy. I took you as more astute than that. This guy wants me dead because I know! Everyone who knows is dead...except for me."

Roselli put down his glass and walked over to him. "Then tell me and we'll stop this guy."

Cogent looked at him and faintly smiled, then turned back and looked out the window. "I'm sure you've tried to get a copy of my book. Did you succeed?"

"Pierce had a copy of part of it."

"Am I ready for a Pulitzer?"

"I don't know. I don't know how it ends."

"Pestilence and death.same as always."

"Let me call that reporter I told you about. You can talk to him, he'll write it any way you want him to." Roselli looked around, spotted the phone and walked over to the bar where it sat. He picked it up, waiting for Cogent to stop him. He didn't...

A New Dawn's Light

It was six thirty when Billy, who had just dozed off, Alex and Pete were awoken by a furious pounding on the front door. It was Al. He had gotten a call from Roselli who had made contact with Cogent. Cogent had requested "the reporter" be brought out to his home.

Al told Billy to get ready fast and asked that Alex and Pete stay behind and wait for his call. This didn't sit too well with Pete. He thought he would be needed to protect his friend. He didn't trust Cogent and he wasn't sure he could trust Roselli to look after Billy the way he would. At least, Al would be with him. There were times that Pete thought of Billy as his little brother and he always believed he was best suited to look out for him.

The irony, here, was that Billy felt the same way about Pete, especially because he had so often shown his own self-destructive tendencies. This was one of those occasions when both men tried to look out for their friend. Eventually, Pete agreed, in part because Billy asked him to, but primarily because Alex had insisted that he heed Roselli's wishes.

It took Billy all of ten minutes to get ready and soon they were driving out to the beach house, Billy quizzing Al as to the exact wording of Roselli's request as they pulled away from the curb. Al couldn't have known and didn't see the old station wagon parked a half block away from Pete's apartment. As he drove his unmarked car down the street, the old station wagon eased its way out into the morning traffic to follow them.

The morning sun was slowly rising over the beach when they turned off Revere Beach Boulevard and onto Oceanview. Billy had never driven out there before and was stunned by the size and grandeur of the homes. Cogent's Tudor was not the nicest on the block but was a beauty, nonetheless. It sat at the end of the street affording it the most spectacular view. Having no idea who he was about to meet, he began to formulate a profile of the unknown man based on the trappings of his lifestyle even though he knew that if Cogent was, indeed, Arliss he was a man to be feared, not envied.

As Al approached the house, the station wagon that had been following pulled over at the end of the street, watching from a distance. Al stopped the car in front of the home, the captain waiting at the front door leaning on a short garden wall that bordered the entranceway. He had his coat off and his shoulder holster was clearly visible as if that was the idea. Billy approached cautiously as Al watched from the car.

Roselli looked up and down the street before his wave sent Al back to Everett. As he turned the car around, he watched Billy for a moment and then accelerated past the parked car as Muir ducked down in the front seat. Once Al had passed, Muir watched the house for a few moments making mental notes as to which house Billy was entering, then he, too, drove back to Everett.

The captain ushered Billy inside the home and led him to the rear deck, where Cogent was waiting for them. At the entrance to the deck, Billy was stunned by the beauty of the bay, the soft gentle breeze and tranquility of the setting. Cogent was sitting on a wicker chair facing away from Billy, ostensibly staring off at the island of Nahant. He noticed two mugs on the table as he and Roselli took seats opposite the unusually subdued man.

Billy reached across the tabletop to shake his hand, but all Cogent did was look at it and then turn away. Roselli started the conversation; "Arthur, this is Billy Petro, the reporter I told you about."

Again, Cogent did not turn his head or make any acknowledgment whatsoever.

He continued; "He'll take down your statement any way you want to make it."

Cogent turned to Billy. "You can handle it?"

"I don't know what it is, yet. But the captain will vouch for my integrity."

"I don't care about your integrity. I just want you to get it straight."

"Arthur, let's just get on with it. I'm willing to bet that none of us got any sleep last night so let's pick up the pace a little."

For the next twenty minutes the three men sat around the table, a skeptical Roselli listening, Billy taking notes and Cogent spinning his tale.

I don't know how and I don't care, but if you have a copy of my manuscript then you know my real name is Arliss and I was once one of the most influential people in the country. I won't bore you with what you've already read, but I know you have some questions about the man you're chasing.

Let me start by telling you his name: Hoffman Muir. Originally, he was an agent in the East German secret police, the Stasi. Ever hear of them? When they were on their own they were more feared than the KGB. There was a single-mindedness to them that made them impossible to deal with in a rational manner.

Anyway, he defected in early '55 and went freelance shortly, thereafter. I suppose, at one time, he was the most highly sought and highly paid assassin in the world. When I was in charge of our South American operations, he was hired on several occasions, mostly to remove business obstacles, maybe an occasional politician.

By the late fifties he had the reputation of a man who could get in and out of anywhere. I don't ever remember him failing. If you needed someone removed, he was the man you would hire. I heard rumors that even the East Germans hired him once. You know, he was freelance so he worked both sides of the fence. What makes him dangerous is that he doesn't care who he hits or why. He gets paid, he does his job.

My people, especially that parasite, Pierce, used to keep me informed of each of his scores. He had an impressive array of hits for a certain family friend in Chicago by the time I needed his services, again.

In early sixty, shortly after Castro closed the casinos and booted out a number of our friends, I was approached to take on the task of coordinating Cuban exile groups in staging a number of clandestine episodes into Cuba. The primary strategy was to keep the pressure on Castro from within. We used the Cuban exiles and our propaganda resources to make sure the situation never got too comfortable in Havana.

Well, as you know, the actual effect was minimal. We decided to try a different tack. We went after him directly and Muir was one of a dozen or so men hired to take on the job. We would slip in an assassin and try to take him out. At first, we didn't use any of the real heavyweights. We underestimated El Presidente. We turned to men like Muir. But, that meddling bastard, Kennedy, couldn't leave well enough alone and put a stop to our plans before we had the best chance to execute them. Muir was never utilized.

You know quite a bit about how things played out, but you don't know the whole story. You believed in Camelot. I never bought that crap. Nothing was better, everything got horribly muddled, confused. Everything we tried to do to get Castro was thwarted. Every operation crushed. He was costing the US billions of dollars, both legit and otherwise. I'm sure you understand.

We put that Communist degenerate in power and then he stole millions of dollars worth of US property and started pointing missiles at us…and that bastard negotiated our right to self-protection right down the drain. Listen, if he wasn't so goddamned popular he would have been considered a traitor. To most of us he was a traitor.

After calling off the hit on Castro, I lost track of him. That was in '62, I think. That was until he surfaced in Dallas the day Kennedy was hit. It doesn't take a rocket scientist to figure out what he was doing there. His signature is a hollow point and, trust me, that's what put the man down…high-powered from directly in front of the bastard's car.

God, when I saw that he was arrested at the scene, I thought something had gone horribly wrong. You know the scenario, Oswald, a commie sympathizer, alone and out of a sense moral righteousness fired the shots. The dumb shit didn't even know he was being used.

Anyway, because he didn't get out of there, Muir was forced to stay out of the country. He was kept out until '74 or '75, something like that. When he returned, he had been replaced by some serious firepower from the West Coast. I hired him a couple of times, but not for any of the big jobs.

By '83 I got word he was looking for me. On a secret trip to Tehran I heard Muir was in the country, so with the help of the Iranian Secret Police I had him picked up. The last I heard was that he died after a month of Iranian hospitality. When I returned to the US the word was that Muir was dead and a lot of people were able to sleep at night.

I don't know how he got out of Tehran, or for that matter when. What I can't believe, is that spiny toad Pierce never told me he had him in tow. I'm sure he knew that would have scared me off and his little enterprise would never have gotten off the ground. You see, Pierce had no contacts, just a lot of dangerous information.

Of course, now he's got what he should've gotten years ago. And I'm next, I'm sure. It's a hell of a way to go out, don't you think?

Billy looked at George Arliss for the first time and saw a frail old man, seemingly aged over a twenty-minute span. A man who thought of himself as the ultimate patriot being stalked by a man much of his own creation.

"Who hired him to kill Kennedy?" Was the first question out of Billy's mouth?

"It doesn't really matter, does it? There were a hundred men with the means who would've paid Muir to take him out. The Exiled Cubans, organized crime, oil interests, it goes on and on. I told you, behind the scenes, there were a lot of angry people in Washington in the sixties."

"And your role?"

"Oh please, do you know how many people knew it was coming. We just didn't know the exact time and place. But, I didn't know ten people who were surprised."

"That doesn't answer my question."

"I had no direct participation, if that's what you mean. I helped with the Oswald myth, but wasn't directly related to a specific event. At least not that I was aware of at the time. Personally, I thought it was going down in Miami a little later on."

Billy was writing as much as he could, as fast as he could. Meanwhile, Roselli sat silently until he had enough of Arliss' self-righteousness. "You are an arrogant SOB, aren't you, Arthur? Thank God most people don't think like you."

"Don't get on your moral high horse, Captain. You're one of those men who sees everything in black and white terms. There's no such world. Everything is drawn in shades, you have to be able to make your own decisions without that moral clarity you so treasure."

"Why do you think he'll get you this time?" Billy wasn't sure they should try to protect him. After all, he had read his file and Arliss was involved in a lot of shady, if not outright illegal actions.

"I did a lot of moving around last night and realized that I can't beat him by myself anymore and most of my so-called friends don't have the stomach to go up against him. Not now, anyways. So, that's how it'll play out."

The sun was full in the sky and there was a soft breeze coming in from the ocean. They could see several people walking the beach, a common practice among the elderly residents of the large condominiums that populated the parcels of land across from the beach. The area in back of Arliss' house was public access, but few people ventured down in that direction, so aside from the residents of the immediate neighborhood the beach was empty.

A disquieting hush had descended on the three men. Billy thought back to Dallas and remembered how he and his mother cried, his dad angry and frustrated. They had all watched the funeral cortege and it was years before Billy could get the sound of that snare drum out of his mind. Even now, he compared every politician to JFK. All of them came up short and he never stopped to try and figure out why.

Billy was done writing. He was too tired and stunned. He stood up and walked to the railing at the edge of the deck. Standing there, he tried to recall the events of November 22nd, 1963. It was all confused, now. Time had rendered it forever gray, more a feeling than an actual event. He remembered how he and his father would discuss the case for conspiracy and how his father couldn't bring himself to admit that powers within the US could actually remove a sitting president.

They both, mistakenly felt that the country felt the same about him, that they all had the utmost confidence in him. It was strange to hear things from Arliss that he had heard whispered by friends who delved much more deeply into the tragedy than he had. Still, he was always a believer. Now, he was ashamed that he wasn't more aware of some of the things that Arliss had mentioned.

His thoughts were interrupted by Roselli. "I had a feeling it wasn't going to be pretty. I'll tell you what, Arthur, if this bastard doesn't get you, I'm gonna take you in, myself!"

"Don't waste your time. More important men than you have tried, in the past."

Billy turned around. "The House Committee on Assassinations?"

"That's one. Nothing I've said can be independently corroborated, so don't waste your energy."

Roselli went into the house and came back out with the portable phone. "Billy, I'll get you a ride back, okay?"

Billy sat back at the table and took a quick look at his notes. "Are we done, here? I'm not sure I don't have some more questions."

Arliss stood up and started for the house, then stopped and looked at Billy. "School's out. You've got more than you can handle, as it is. Besides, I can see you're not going to do me justice. Don't be so quick to wrap yourself up in your precious flag if you aren't prepared to make the kinds of sacrifices that I've had to make in my lifetime. Now, I need some time to get some things in order."

He went inside, leaving Billy and Roselli standing on his deck staring at each other. "I'll call Al to come and get you."

"Call Pete, he's chomping at the bit to get out of that apartment. He'll ride along with Al, if you don't mind."

"I do. I don't want him messing with Arliss. I was serious about bringing him in. I don't know on what charges, but I want his story in some official record."

"He'll never co-operate. He's right. I'll write this up and people will just chalk it up to another conspiracy freak churning up some new dirt."

Roselli dialed Pete's number, told him to get Al and come and get Billy.

The Longest Ride

Al was waiting outside Pete's apartment when Roselli called. Much to Alex's disapproval they went off to pick up Billy. It was getting close to Rush Hour, the traffic picking up as they left Everett and headed towards the beach. Pete asked Al why he sat outside rather than coming in and waiting, there.

Al just laughed. "When are you going to open your sorry eyes and make Alex the happy woman she deserves to be? Though, if you ask me, she deserves better than you!"

Pete stared out the window and mumbled something under his breath.

"What did you say?" Al enjoyed seeing him flustered.

"Let's just get this over with. You can worry about me after we get Billy back and find out who this Cogent guy really is. Is that too much to ask?"

For the rest of the ride they sat in silence, watching the day take shape, get in its normal rhythm. They rode through traffic, past crowded bus stops and, once in Revere, past the Commuter train line that ran behind the Dog track. Everywhere they rode, life was humming along oblivious to what was going on in a beachfront house right in their backyard.

It took them almost twenty minutes, but they pulled up in front of the large Tudor shortly after Billy had gone outside to wait. He had said his good-byes, after trying to get a few more questions answered. Arliss was done talking, except to say that he intended to deny everything Billy had if he survived, instead of Muir.

Roselli was staying behind, deciding that he had a better chance of stopping the assassin without the help of the Revere police, something Al had warned him against. Al knew enough not to press the issue, so he dropped it. Once back in the car, he told his friends that he was going to sneak back once he had delivered them to the newspaper office.

Both Al and Pete wanted to know what they talked about. Billy told them that he admitted to being Arliss and then went on to tell them all that he had said. Al was livid and wanted to go back to "take the sucker out!" While Pete sat quietly with his thoughts for most of the trip.

After Billy finished his tale he, too, was done talking and they completed the ride back in silence. These three men had known each other for thirty years and they had never taken a ride with as much tension in the air. They had seen most of the worst that life can throw at you and never had they had a ride anything like this one. In fact, even though they were back in Everett in a little over fifteen minutes, it seemed as though they had traveled for hours.

Al left them off at the Gazette, Alex already there, briefing Fox and Claire. They weren't even in the door by the time Al had screeched away from the curb and headed back to Arliss' house.

The Story of a Lifetime

Billy and Pete sat down at one of the desks. Alex walked over to them as they looked sullen and distant. "Where the hell have you been?" She asked Billy.

"That's a good way of putting it. I feel like I spent an eternity with the devil." He looked at Fox. "You were right, that guy was Arliss. He's a former power mad agency hack who talks like he's the only one who knows what patriotism is all about."

"What did he tell you?"

"Simply put, our mystery man is a trained assassin by the name of Hoffman Muir and that he's after Arliss. All this has been because he's been after Arliss. Apparently, several years ago Arliss tried to have him killed...thought he was dead, mind you. Until he showed up, here."

"And the smuggling operation?"

"Muir has nothing to do with it. Fifteen years ago, Arliss turned this guy over to the Iranian secret police and thought he died while in their midst. Well, obviously, he didn't, but Arliss didn't know it. Now, Muir wants to return the favor. That's Arliss' spin on what's going on."

Pete looked over at Billy. "Poor Blake, he had no idea."

"No, I doubt that he did."

"Billy, tell them the rest."

"The rest?" Alex had been listening and wasn't sure she wanted to hear any more.

"Muir really is the man on the grassy knoll and guys like Arliss put him there! Says it was the patriotic thing to do!"

"Arliss planned or was a part of the conspiracy."

"He says he wasn't, except that he helped create the 'Oswald myth'."

Fox stared out the window. "Of course. Pierce was working under Arliss when he gave that phony story about Oswald being in Mexico City."

"Where was Al going in such a rush?" Alex didn't like the way he took off. She was concerned that there was no one outside to protect them and concerned that Al looked angry and maybe, out of control.

"Going back. Roselli stayed behind."

*****

For the next hour Billy and Fox carefully reconstructed the tale that Arliss had spun. Fox, with help from Alex and Claire tried, as best he could, to verify whatever aspects of the story they could find on the Net. Most of what they found were historical notes with no specific mention of Arliss or anyone else, who could corroborate his story.

As Billy finished up, there was considerable debate about what to do with the story. Fox suggested that they contact some friends in

Boston or Washington and try to get the story some national attention. Because of the volatile nature of the story, Billy wanted to keep it more low key.

Meanwhile, Pete was walking around the office like a caged beast. He kept telling them that they should try to contact Al and find out what was going on. Finally, tired of listening to him complain, Fox told him to try to make contact.

Pete tried the number Al had given them, but there was no answer. He didn't mention anything to the rest. He didn't want to upset them, especially, Alex. After trying the number three or four times he dialed the direct number for the Everett station house and tried to locate either Al or Roselli.

As Pete was calling the station, the phone rang. Claire answered it. The call came from the police informing them of a break-in at 53 Tremont Street, near the Malden line. She passed the information on, but Billy was preoccupied with his writing as Pete got off the phone and told them that they had to drop what they were doing and head over to Roselli's house. There had been a break-in.

Red Herring

Pete and Billy had to take the car Fox had been leasing to drive over to Roselli's house.

There were three squad cars and an unmarked vehicle already there. They got out and asked if Roselli or Al were around, but neither was there. The officer in charge told Billy that the alarm had sounded about fifteen minutes ago and that when they got there they found the back door open and the living room trashed. By the nature of the vandalism it looked as though it was kids.

Billy asked how the kids could have gotten out of the house fast enough to avoid the police, but he had no explanation saying that they must have reacted to the alarm by trashing what they could and then took off. He doubted that they would have had enough time to actually steal anything.

Pete asked around about whether or not someone had gotten a hold of Roselli. He was told that they had had some initial trouble, but that he was on his way. When he asked about Al, the officer didn't know if they had even tried to contact him since he wasn't on duty, yet.

Within a few minutes, another unmarked car approached. When it stopped, out stepped Roselli, who immediately ran into the house. Al got out of the driver's side and walked over to Billy.

Billy asked; "How'd he know you were there?"

"He didn't. When I saw him run out of the house, I pulled out and he got in."

"What about Arliss?"

"I told the captain I would stay behind, but he said that it wouldn't be right. We called the Revere police and they said they would send a car around to check on him."

"Do you think that's a good idea?"

"No, but..."

As he was saying this Roselli came running out of the house, straight for Al's car. He jumped in and sped off. Al ran to the house and went inside. The living room was the only room that had sustained any damage. The TV was pulled onto the floor and the stereo system cabinet had been toppled over.

Al approached one of the officers and asked what had transpired. The officer said that he walked in, looked over the damage and then picked up a broken picture frame from the floor underneath the stereo cabinet. That picture was now lying on the coffee table. It was a picture of Roselli and his deceased wife. Whoever knocked it over had torn Roselli's head from the picture.

The officer asked; "Is that some sort of message, Sergeant?"

Al thought for a moment, then; "Roselli sure thinks it is!"

Pete and Billy had moved to the front of the house, but none of the officers would let them enter. Al came out and asked Billy if they had a car. Billy showed him the keys and he told them that they had to get to Revere fast.

Patriot's Day

Billy gave the keys to Al and they piled in, Al barely waiting for Pete to jump into the back before peeling out. On the way to Arliss's Al told them what was in the house and they agreed that Roselli got the intended message.

Traffic was heavier than it had been in the morning so it took them longer to get there. When they turned the corner onto Oceanview they could see Roselli's car was half on the curb, half on the street the front door still open.

They approached cautiously. From the street they could see that the front door to the Tudor was also open. Al pulled the car to the curb a couple of houses before Arliss's.

Al tried to get both of them to stay with the car, but he knew that was fruitless. He warned them to stay in back of him as he pulled out his service revolver and moved towards the house. He reached the front door and said he could smell gasoline. Pete said it was the same smell he picked up at Bonner before the building became engulfed in flames.

With a sense of renewed urgency Al ran into the house. He heard some commotion from the back of the house and ran to the noise. He got to edge of the deck and found Arliss lying in a pool of blood. He bent over and felt for a pulse, but could find none.

Downstairs, Billy saw that the sliding glass door from the living room was open. He walked to it and looked outside in the back yard. He heard a low moaning sound. It was Roselli. He and Pete ran to the captain who was still alive, having been hit in the shoulder area. He was bleeding heavily, but was conscious.

"Where's Al or the Revere police?"

Billy called out to Al who was on the deck above them. He looked over and jumped down. He came over to Roselli.

"Don't let him get away, again! I came right at him, he was going to ignite the place. I may have hit him, but he got off a burst of fire and before I knew it I felt like my arm was being torn out of its socket. Go after him, but be careful, he's got more than one weapon."

Pete had climbed to the deck, saw Arliss and looked off down the beach.

“I bet that’s him running towards the boulevard. Ask the captain if he hit him, he looks like he’s dragging his left leg!”

Billy ran up to see what Pete was looking at while Al called in an “Officer down alert”. Then, he too, went up onto the deck.

“I’ll follow him on foot. You tell the cruiser, when it gets here where I am.”

As he started to go over the side, Pete grabbed him by the arm. “No way, man. You cut him off, we’ll flush him to your position, then you can make the grab.”

“No way! You have got to stay here!”

Billy yelled at the two to stop bickering, because Muir was already at the boulevard beyond the beach and was crossing. He could see two cars collide as Muir stepped out in front of them brandishing a pistol. Billy hopped down onto the beach, the fall a little longer than he expected and then yelled up at Pete to follow. Pete ran down the stairs and opened the gate, catching up to Billy within a few steps.

Al ran out the front of the house and got into the unmarked car that Roselli left at the curb, peeled out, making a U-turn in front of the house and heading off towards Muir's last position. Al reached the boulevard before either Billy or Pete, but as he did he could see Muir disappearing down a driveway into a backyard.

The row of houses that bordered the beach was in a low-lying area that had marshland behind them and a major road beyond that. Al screeched to a stop and turned his car around, knowing that if he let him get to the highway he would be gone before they could stop him.

As Al turned the car around, Pete and Billy finally reached the street. They ran across and followed Muir into the back yard. Muir kicked open a gate that led from the backyard to a wooden walkway across the marsh. He could see the road and freedom no more than a hundred yards away.

He managed to get almost halfway across before looking back and seeing Pete and Billy about to get on the walkway. He turned, kneeled and fired two shots, grazing a fencepost and splashing the water in front of Pete. Billy dove behind the stone column to safety.

Pete was carrying a sidearm and drew it out, intending to fire, but as Muir got back on his feet he threw the pistol into the marsh and pulled on the automatic that was slung over his back and fired off a quick sustained burst. Pete dove into the marsh as the bullets ricocheted off the wooden planking, taking off the tops of the weeds that surrounded the walkway.

Billy held his ears and stayed right where he was, while Pete crouched in knee-deep water, feeling the muck at the bottom of the marsh ooze into his sneakers. Muir was firing blindly and trying to walk at the same time. His left leg was bleeding and he was having a hard time maneuvering along the unsteady walkway. By the time he was within ten yards of the roadway he was out of ammunition so he threw that gun into the marsh as well.

As Muir was about to get off the walkway, Al had jumped the center barrier and came screeching to a stop on the sidewalk right in front of Muir. Al had his gun out and was shouting for him to stop. Muir jumped into the muck and tried to make his way across the marsh to one of the other backyards.

Al fired a warning shot, but it didn't slow Muir down. He relentlessly forged through the reeds, tearing them out of his way as he made his way to a stonewall that bordered the house next to the one where Billy, and now Pete were standing. Al had come halfway down the walkway, not wanting to fire on Muir, possibly killing him and losing him forever.

Once Muir reached the wall, Al shouted at him one last time. When he didn't pay any attention, Al fired two shots as Muir pulled himself up onto the wall and then fell over it into the backyard. Al ran down the planking as Billy and Pete ran into the yard.

Muir had been hit and had fallen into a pile of leaves and yard debris that had been raked against the wall. When they arrived he was lying on his side wheezing. Billy got to him first.

He pulled Muir over onto his back when he saw the gun. Muir had concealed it beneath him, his right arm pinned against his side. He stared right into Billy's eyes, then smiled as...

The whole side of his body exploded before he could squeeze the trigger as Pete unloaded three quick shots into his torso. Blood spurted from his mouth as the third shot hit its mark, the blood draining from his face, his eyes rolling up into his head.

Billy froze, staring at the dead man, his hands and the front of his jacket covered in Muir's blood as Al put a hand on Billy's shoulder. He knelt down and checked for a pulse. He didn't expect to find one and he didn't. Then he stood up and took the smoking gun from Pete's hands. The three men stood there staring at Muir.

Suddenly, Billy looked at Pete. "Do you know what today is?"

"Saturday?"

"You ass. It's Patriot's Day. They're probably getting ready to start the marathon right around now."

"I'll be damned…the Shot Heard 'Round the World."

By now, there were several people milling about. Two Revere officers came running into the yard as the din from people talking, yelling and running began to escalate. Al identified, himself, and the officers called for an ambulance, the coroner would not be far behind. A second Revere squad car stopped at the top of the street and Roselli got out, his arm in a sling and one of the officers helping him down the driveway to where Billy, Pete and Al were standing by the body.

Pete looked up and he and Al walked over to assist the captain who had insisted on seeing Muir's lifeless body before heading off to the hospital. When Pete grabbed his arm, he looked at him and shook his head. In a shaky voice, fighting to catch his breath, he smiled and said; "I knew you'd be in the middle of this."

"Couldn't let you down, now, could I?"

Epilogue

Six Months Later

Al and Pete were seated at a back booth in Coda's talking about the day's happenings. It had been six months since the deaths of Hoffman Muir and George Arliss. The city had returned to the quiet patterns of life that had formerly punctuated most everyone's existence, here. They were waiting for Alex and Billy.

Billy ended up writing a series of articles for one of the big Boston Dailies, outlining the four days of terror that Muir had brought to Everett, touching, only briefly on the killer's connection to the JFK assassination. Now, he was employed in Boston, working on a series of articles about cost overruns at the new Deer Island Sewage Treatment Plant.

Alex arrived and the friends greeted each other. She had a heavy book under her arm and when she sat down she put it in the middle of the table. It was "A Life in the Shadows" by George Arliss, forward by Billy Petro.

"Where is he, anyway?" Asked Alex.

"Why would you ask that? He's always late, now that he has a real job." Replied Al.

"I know he's better off, but I miss just being able to walk into the Gazette and hang around." Pete did miss his friend.

"Did Fox throw your ass out?" Asked Al.

Pete ignored Al. "Did you read it?"

Alex smiled and excitedly turned to the front of the book. She paged to the very beginning, to: Forward by William "Billy" Petro.

I'm not sure what I can add to the following tale of greed and power gone awry, but this much is clear, there are men like George Arliss and they have considerable power in this country...and they always have. What may not be easily apparent is the depth and lengths these men will go to in order to maintain that power.

As you read the following pages, try to keep in mind that at some warped level these men believe themselves to be patriots. In fact, the first time I met George Arliss, the day of his own assassination, he told me a tale, so outrageous as to leave me thinking that these men are capable of anything. Yet, he assured me that what was done, was done in the name of patriotism.

We met in the early morning hours, just after dawn, in an upscale Tudor home overlooking the ocean. We settled down and spoke for the next half hour as he spun his tale. I took notes though most of his story seemed too incredulous to be true. That was until I read the rest of this book.

Continue from here at your own risk, knowing that it's best to know what these men are up to and that behind every facade of power these men hide in the shadows.

She closed the book and looked at her two friends.

"It's about time he had something in print." Al said with a wide smile.

As he said this in walked Billy. Disheveled from his tiresome commute, tonight an hour affair. He knew what table to go to and soon he was seated amongst his friends. He saw the book.

"What do you think…too melodramatic?"

"As always." Pete took another sip from the coffee cup in front of him. They all laughed, just as they always did in the old days.

Times hadn't really changed. Sure, Billy was now working in Boston, but Alex still taught at the High School, Pete still did whatever it was he did, Al continued to patrol the streets of Everett and Fox and Claire still ran the Post Gazette. Billy wrote a weekend feature for the paper.

Roselli had recovered from his wounds and was even more disagreeable than ever, but the venom was gone, especially with Pete. Oh they still went at it, but the passion was gone. As for Blake, he was still recovering, not yet well enough to return to work. The irony of America's Front Page doing a story on Billy, Pete and Al not lost on Blake's fragile ego.

Billy didn't really appreciate the notoriety, not the way Pete had. But deep down he felt a new energy, a desire to finally go forward, a need to test himself to find out how good he really was. In the end he reconciled the old demons, finally, understanding that he had always been a damn fine reporter.

About the Author

The Shooter is the first novel by Vincent Simonelli. With a degree in film studies from the University of Miami, he has written two screenplays, a sitcom and several short stories. A life-long Bostonian, he writes affectionately of his hometown, working at one of the large Universities for which the city is justifiably famous. He expects to publish the sequel to the Shooter, The Solar Antiquities, in early 2004. He is married, the father of a young son and is presently completing the third novel in this series.

Printed in the United States
23247LVS00001B/79

9 781410 709516